YELLOW FEVER

Other Stories by Richard Braden

YELLOW FEVER

The 1849 California Gold Rush

Richard Braden

iUniverse, Inc.
New York Lincoln Shanghai

Yellow Fever
The 1849 California Gold Rush

iUniverse books may be ordered through booksellers or by contacting:

iUniverse
2021 Pine Lake Road, Suite 100
Lincoln, NE 68512
www.iuniverse.com
1-800-Authors (1-800-288-4677)

This book is a work of fiction. Names, characters, and incidents are products of the author's imagination. Any resemblance to actual events or persons, living or dead, is entirely coincidental.

Front cover artwork by Orrel Schooler, Centennial, CO.

ISBN-13: 978-0-595-38109-8 (pbk)
ISBN-13: 978-0-595-82476-2 (ebk)
ISBN-10: 0-595-38109-X (pbk)
ISBN-10: 0-595-82476-5 (ebk)

Printed in the United States of America

Acknowledgements

My thanks to Ranger Mark Michalski, Marshall Gold Discovery State Park, Coloma, CA, for his searches into the details of the City of Coloma and County of Eldorado day-to-day operations and local businesses as they existed in 1849.

I am also indebted to Dr. Richard Allen, a Cherokee Nation Policy Analyst, Tahlequah, Oklahoma, who read this text and pointed out numerous errors in the first draft. Hopefully these have all been corrected.

Bob Schantz of spanishlake.com, St. Croix, Wisconsin, told me all about Morgan Horses and horseshoeing as it existed in the 1840s.

Esther McCrumb of the South Platte Valley Historical Society showed me what remains of Fort Lupton. If she has her way, the fort will be rebuilt some day.

Introduction

This is a story about a Cherokee family who survived forced displacement from Georgia to the northeastern corner of the 'Indian Territory' (now Oklahoma) by the U.S. Army in the late 1830s and now seeks more farming land and better opportunities in the headwaters of the Arkansas River in the late 1840s. Their motivation was simple—the U. S. Congress had driven them out of their ancestral home along the Atlantic Ocean with a stroke of a pen, so what assurance did the Cherokees have that they could keep the 'new land' in the Indian Territory promised to them by the federal government?

In 1838 The U. S. Cavalry escorted the first contingent of Cherokees from North Carolina and Georgia and dropped them off in the Cherokee Nation Territory just as winter was setting in. Four thousand Indians died along the route and many more perished shortly after their arrival in the new land. The Simmons family survived, but barely.

Eleven years later the family decided to search for farmland in the extreme western part of the Kansas Territory (close to the Rocky Mountains) but this search yielded disappointing results initially. Then their entire outlook was changed when the word came over the Rocky Mountains from the west that gold has been discovered in huge quantities on public land in central California. The Simmons family knew a lot about gold mining, and was tempted to mine for the elusive yellow metal again.

From their vantage point in Fort Lupton, Kansas Territory (now Colorado), on the South Platte River, they found themselves 900 miles from their home in the Cherokee Nation Territory and 900 miles from the gold fields of Sutter's Mill.

They had a big decision to make, and they made it quickly—they headed west for California, across the most unforgiving stretch of land anywhere in North America.

Arnest Simmons is the leader of the five-person group. He is 44 years old and is a member of the Cherokee Nation Council. His wife, Jean, is five years younger than he. They have two unmarried sons, Renwe and Staufo, ages 21 and 17. They also have two daughters, Eileen and Marcy, ages 20 and 18, who are married to Cherokee men and live within a few miles of the Simmons farm just south of Joplin, Missouri. The Simmons made a living by selling vegetables in the Joplin market.

Jean's older brother, Howey Tremaine, is included in the group that goes west to find farming land—he is the oldest person in the group. His wife, Claire, plans to go west with him but she changes her mind when she discovers how difficult the trip will be. She also has a demanding job in the community as a second-grade school teacher. Howey and Claire Tremaine have no children.

The trip to the headwaters of the Arkansas River was made a little easier because the five people in the group (Arnest, Jean, Renwe, Staufo, and Howey) have Morgan horse-mixes to ride on—ten horses for the five people. The Morgan horses were part of a trade made in 1828 when the family sold its gold claim at Licklog (now Dahlonega, Georgia) to a man from Kentucky. The sale price was $100.00 and a Morgan stallion. Arnest wanted the stallion, so Jean and Howey, his partners, split the $100.00.

This trip to the west in search of more farmland was the first such trip for Renwe and Staufo. They were born after the Licklog gold rush of 1828, and they didn't want to miss any part of this present adventure. The Simmons girls and their husbands offered to tend to the Simmons farmland while they were gone.

And so it was that in late April 1849 the five Cherokees set out for Fort Bent, a trading post on the Santa Fe Trail, only 100 miles from the Rocky Mountains. The Cherokees had a written language to accompany their spoken language, thanks to a scholar named Sequoyah. The language had been published only twenty years earlier, but already most Cherokee school children knew how to write in the Cherokee Nation language. There were two Cherokee newspapers that published weekly to inform all Cherokees about what was going on in the world around them. Staufo was given the job of 'family scribe' on this trip, and most of what you read below was taken from his scribbled notes, as amended by his mother, Jean.

This is their story.

CHAPTER 1

Westward Ho

No one in the Simmons family was sure who was the first to suggest that they go west and look for more farmland. The lands to the west were not nearly as fertile as the land they presently occupied, but there was a lot more of it. The Cherokee Nation property consisted of over seven million acres in the north-east corner of what was known at that time as the 'Indian Territory'. All the land was owned by the Cherokee Nation, but the seven clans within the Nation had apportioned the land to their families for farming. A family owned the improvements to their land, but never the land itself.

The local rainfall in the new land supported the vegetable crops that they grew in the spring and early summer, but their farm was too far away from a major river to irrigate the fields. 'Dry land farming' is a highly speculative business. The 700+ acres that they farmed allowed them to raise a small herd of beef cattle, and most of the beef was sold on the market.

There were lots of rumors about free land in the newly-opened western frontier. When the Mexican government ceded all its land west of the Louisiana Purchase in 1847 to the USA (at the end of the Mexican War), land became available in the Kansas, Nebraska, and Oregon Territories. Rumor had it that the Oregon Territory was more fertile than the Kansas and Nebraska Territories, but the trek to the Pacific Northwest was a difficult one. A lot of emigrants died trying to reach Oregon.

The Missouri Territory had filled up fast with farmers and ranchers, and Missouri was already a state in the Union. Farther to the west, in the Kansas and Nebraska Territories, the buildup of families was much slower—due primarily to the lack of water in these parts and the presence of the Plains Indians, who had occupied these lands for centuries. The Plains Indians were discovering that the white man intended to occupy all of the West, and there would be little if any space left for the present owners. If they knew anything about past history they would have realized what had happened to the 'Five Civilized Tribes' in the East was now happening to them.

The decision was made to plant the spring vegetable crops before the group departed for the west. After planting, the family waited for the arrival of the early May rains—if the rains did not come then re-planting would be necessary four weeks later. The rains came, right on schedule.

❈   ❈   ❈

The trip west from the northeast corner of the Cherokee Nation Territory to Bent's Fort in the Kansas Territory (near the headwaters of the Arkansas River) began with a 320 mile trek west-northwest to Dodge City and the Santa Fe Trail. This part of the trip took only nine days, despite the fact that the family had to find its own way across the southern strip of the Kansas Territory. Very few groups made this trek, so the family had to depend on a crude map that they had purchased in Tahlequah and 'dead reckoning'. So long as the sun shone it was easy to find which direction was west.

In Dodge City the Simmons got their first chance to see the 'real west' as the eastern newspapers described it. Dodge City was a collecting point for cattle on their way to the eastern markets. The 'iron horse' was already there in Dodge City, ready to take carload after carload of cattle to Chicago, St Louis, Memphis, Philadelphia, New York City, and all points east. To the west of Dodge City there was a thousand miles of plains inhabited by bison and the Plains Indians.

Dodge City wasn't nearly as big as Joplin, Missouri, but it had all the hustle-bustle of a big town on the prairie. The people who settled the western towns soon discovered that the greatest natural enemy they faced was 'fire', either man-made or fire created by lightning strikes. They learned to spread-out the town with large gaps between buildings so, when one building burned down the adjacent buildings would survive. The great fear of fire extended to most commercial businesses—so the buildings were generally unheated and terribly cold (potbelly stoves had not become popular at this time in the west). There were notable exceptions of course—the saloons and honky-tonks were all built around large open fireplaces that invited prospective customers inside, to get away from the cold. These structures burned down frequently, and were always rebuilt.

It was good that the Cherokees did not need to replenish their supplies in Dodge City because Indians (any kind of Indians) were not entirely welcome in town. So the family, sensing some hostility, chose to remain west of the town and close to the Arkansas River, where other emigrant groups were camped, preparing for the move west.

They rested in the Dodge City area for one day and began following the Arkansas River west. The Santa Fe Trail was not crowded—there were an equal number of groups on horseback and in wagon trains. There were even a few hearty individuals pushing 'pushcarts'. The wagon trains were lucky to make twenty miles a day with their oxen pulling the wagons and their cattle grazing along the trail, but a group on horseback could cover 35 to 40 miles a day. This is not to say that a person could ride a horse for forty miles—the rider had to walk with the horse for part of the day so the horse could regain its stamina. This was especially true during the heat of the day when the sun bore down on the travelers on the trail.

The Santa Fe Trail was well marked. The iron-clad wheels of conestoga wagons, buckboards, and stage coaches cut a definitive trail across the plains. When an emigrant group decided to quit for the day there were lots of chores to perform before the sun went down. There were animals to water and feed, wagon wheels and hubs to inspect for excessive wear, creation of a temporary corral to restrain the livestock until the next morning, food to be prepared, and assignments among the men in the group to stand guard throughout the night. These guards had no trouble remaining awake at their posts—the unsubstantiated stories about Indian attacks and groups of marauders who terrorized the plains were fresh in their minds.

The Simmons had the same duties to perform every evening, and they were only five in number. They split the overnight guard duties between the four men, and Jean did all the cooking. Every evening she conducted a search in the immediate camp area for food—mostly bird's eggs because eggs were a delicacy on the trail and they could not be preserved for more than a few hours. The boys, Renwe and Staufo, helped her in this evening search. The Cherokees had no milk, and no one in the group drank coffee. If they wanted something hot to drink, Jean would cut-up some of the dried fruit that she carried on her pack horse into very small pieces and heat water with the fruit. It could pass for a fruit drink if you were not too picky. The most important feature of the drink was that it was hot.

Jean had a favorite nanny goat at the farm that could have provided some milk on the trip, and Jean would have brought her had they not been traveling on horseback. If they had brought a wagon, the nanny goat would have made the trip also—inside the wagon. There was no way a nanny goat could walk the 800 or so miles to the Rocky Mountains, playing catch-up with ten Morgan horses.

Jean carried about fifty pounds of beef and pork jerky on her pack horse, cut into thin strips. The jerky was made by pounding spices into the meat with an awl. Then it was salted, dried, and smoked. Jerky was the only food consumed during the day since the group never stopped for a noon meal. If a person got hungry they could munch on the jerky. Each person was allocated eight ounces of jerky a day; it was placed in the saddlebags along with the black powder horn and ball ammunition for their weapons. Renwe and Staufo had a habit of eating all their jerky early in the day, but no one complained if Jean gave them more, because the two boys were still growing. They needed more food than the elder members of the family.

Beside jerky, their diet consisted of smoked bacon (which Jean cooked every night), small quantities of Irish potatoes, sweet potatoes, onions, dried beans, and turnips. Jean also carried a few packs of soda crackers that could be eaten with the jerky. If anyone had a problem with constipation, Jean had dried apples, persimmons, and apricots. The dried apricots worked the best.

After Jean cooked the bacon, she took some of the bacon fat out of the skillet, mixed it with dry flour, and prepared biscuits. The biscuits were cooked in the frying pan also. Jean always added a little cane sugar to the biscuits to enhance their flavor. Water was their only drink, and they got this from their canteens that Arnest had purchased in Tahlequah shortly before they left the farm. The first few days of their trip, finding water to refill the canteens in the evening was difficult because the family had to cut their own trail from Tahlequah to Dodge City, where they met the Arkansas River. They had to keep an eye out for water sources because there were very few north-south streams in the southern Kansas Territory. There was no water shortage after they reached the Arkansas River, however. Every morning, as they broke camp on the river's edge, every water container was filled for the day.

Most wagon trains carried wooden barrels for water. The water barrel had a spigot on one side and it was usually bound to the wagon with rawhide strips. But the Cherokees had no wagon, and no water barrels. Instead, they had small leather water bags that held about two gallons of water each. The water bags were stored directly behind the saddle, at the same place where the saddlebags were kept. They were intended to be an emergency water supply.

The Cherokees had two kinds of firearms—two flintlock rifles, model 1813, .54 caliber, and five Allen & Thurber six-shot, .36 caliber pepperboxes. The group had owned the two flintlock rifles for years; they were used for game-hunting. But the pepperboxes were new, purchased in Joplin only a week before the party left for the West. Pepperboxes were the most popular and the cheapest handguns in America at the time. They cost only $10.00 each, one-third of what an early Colt revolver cost. All the Colt weapons were in short supply.

Before the group left home, Arnest set up a target-practice area behind the barn and everyone had a chance to fire their new sidearm. The pepperbox had six barrels that were loaded from the muzzle end with black powder, a lead ball, and finally a cotton wad to keep everything in the barrel. At the breech end a percussion cap was placed over a small firing hole in the barrel. The action of the trigger caused the barrels to rotate every time the trigger was pulled.

The problem with the pepperboxes was their range—you couldn't count on hitting anything past twenty feet of so. But what they lacked in accuracy they made up for in noise, smoke, and confusion. Since all the flintlock and percussion weapons had a 'firing hole' at the rear of the breach, the person who fired the weapon was always covered with black smoke and particles of burning gun powder as soon as the trigger was pulled. With the flintlock rifles, the family had learned to close their eyelids as the trigger was pulled—to keep burning particles of black powder from coating their eyeballs.

As they traveled, the Cherokees kept one of the rifles at the head of the party and one at the rear, for group defense. At no time was either of these weapons fired in anger.

The group carried the standard medical kit of the day—gauze, tape, iodine, a tourniquet, a pink-colored powder that helped settle one's stomach, and a metal container of salve for burns and small wounds. Pain killers in a bottle hadn't been invented yet, but the group kept pieces of dried leaves and bark from the willow tree to decrease pain—the patient would chew on the leaves and bark to get the pain ingredient into his/her system.

Every night they had to prepare a temporary corral for their ten horses. Two of their younger animals had a habit of wandering away, and the temporary corral made from ropes and tree branches didn't always keep them close. So these animals had to be 'hobbled' every night with a piece of stiff rawhide that was tied between the animal's two front legs.

It was easy to find firewood every evening, and the first thing that Renwe and Staufo were instructed to do was to get the fire going. They each had a tinderbox that contained small spirals of dried softwood, and the tinderbox was opened for only a few seconds while a 'finger's worth' of tinder was removed. Most tinderboxes started out as containers for pipe tobacco because the lid on pipe tobacco cans always fit tightly on the bottom half of the metallic box. The person starting the fire either rotated a stick fitted with small pieces of flint into a depression in a stone, or stroked a smooth stone with a large piece of flint. Either way, the flint caused small sparks to fall on the tinder and the tinder eventually caught fire.

The tiny fire was aided by the human fire starter who blew gently on the tinder until a fire was established. Now it was time to feed the fire with larger pieces of dry wood until a sizeable fire was burning in a fire pit. If the fire went out the fire starter had to start all over again.

The principal enemy of the fire starter was moisture—any liquid that would keep the tinder from bursting into flame. Starting a fire in a driving rain was absolutely impossible, and everyone knew it. As a result, on the evenings when a fire was needed the most (because everyone was soaked to the skin by driving rains) the chances of starting a fire were nil.

The group had small tents to sleep in, but they seldom erected the tents unless it was going to rain significantly. Then, if they got a fire going, one of the tents would be set close to the fire so a few burning embers could be dragged into the tent to keep a fire going all through the night. The fire was always small because the group of five did not want to bring attention to themselves—a big fire might draw a crowd, which was the last thing the family wanted.

Jean always kept some of the grease that came from the cooking of the smoked bacon in the evening so she could make biscuits early the next morning. If the fire was lost during the night she resorted to handing out old biscuits that were left over from a previous meal. There wasn't time to start a new fire early in the morning.

Getting up in the morning and getting on the trail was always a high-stress time for all because there were so many chores to perform and so little time to do them. The saddles and bridles were removed from the horses every evening, along with the saddle blankets, saddlebags, and waterbags—the horses needed the night to regain their strength for the next day's travel. Then all the leather had to be put back on the horses, usually in the dark. By the time the sun came up the Simmons were well along the trail toward the West.

CHAPTER 2

Bison

The first two week's travel from home to the Indian Lands of the Kansas Territory was easy riding for the Cherokee family—no mountains or large rivers to cross. The Kansas Territory was incredibly long, east to west; it began at Kansas City and Independence and terminated at the Rocky Mountains. During the day they seldom stopped to view the scenery or paused to hunt for game—the trek was all business from daybreak to sundown.

When the group stopped for the evening and set-up camp, it was a different story. In the evening Renwe would hunt for small game close to the campsite, and about every third night he shot jackrabbits, fox, or prairie dogs (It was Lewis and Clark who had named the small plains rodents 'prairie dogs'. Some people thought they should have been named 'prairie rats' because they were close cousins to the eastern rat. But the little rodents shall forever be called 'prairie dogs').

The family had read stories about the giant herds of bison who roamed the West. There were no pictures in the newspapers in those days, but the people who wrote the stories found words to describe these huge, furry animals. The articles pointed out that the animals could be dangerous if one got too close to them. Some of the bulls weighed as much as eighteen hundred pounds.

Six days after the Cherokees left Dodge City they were traveling in single-file through high grass that stood two to three feet tall—adjacent to the deeply rutted trail. Mixed into the tall grass were hundreds of the small prairie dogs. The family followed the Santa Fe Trail closely, but did not remain immediately on the trail because the sod was so hard and the heavy wagons had cut deep, narrow furrows in the trail, making it easy for a horse to twist a hoof. It rained that day, late in the afternoon. The rainfall was heavy but it only lasted for a few minutes before the rainclouds moved east. The rain was refreshing, and it kept their skin damp, but the humidity when the rain stopped was stifling.

Then, Staufo, who was bringing up the rear, spotted something moving toward them from the north, separating the high grass as it came their way. He called out quickly, and pointed to the north. Sure enough, there was some kind of a large animal (or animals) headed their way. The Simmons weren't sure what to do, so Arnest told the group to form in a tight circle until these animals passed by.

No one was sure what the animals were, but from the size of the swath they were creating, it must be bison. "Get in here tight," Arnest called out in a low-pitched voice. "Staufo, get ready to fire your flintlock if the animals get too close." Staufo nodded to show that he got the message. As the animals came closer, Arnest turned to Staufo and added, "But don't shoot unless the animals are headed right for us. We don't want to shoot an animal and then have to leave it out here on the prairie to die."

Now Staufo was disappointed. If he got close to a bison why in the world couldn't he shoot it? It wasn't as if the plains were just about out of these animals—the newspapers reported that there were thousands of them on the central plains.

When the bison came within 100 yards of the Cherokees they split-off to their left and passed behind the Cherokee group. There were bulls and cows and yearlings, all moving at a gentle gallop, about ten or twelve of them. When they passed, Staufo asked: "When do I get to shoot one of these animals?" Arnest replied with "as soon as we need the meat. We have plenty of food right now."

That evening, when Jean was starting to make biscuits, Staufo and Howey headed out to the north with the two flintlock rifles. They promised to be back within the hour with fresh meat. Over the next 45 minutes the group at the campsite heard three gunshots, and the men showed up a few minutes later with a jackrabbit and a prairie dog. The jackrabbit was good eating, but the prairie dog was too fatty. "Next time we're going to shoot a pronghorn deer," Staufo commented. He should wish! It would be at least another 300 miles before a deer or elk of any kind was spotted by the group.

Morale was high in the family. The animals had plenty of grass to eat and water to drink. The middle of the day was oppressively hot, but by two hours before sundown the plains cooled. At night there was a breeze, and sometimes it became necessary to cover yourself with a saddle blanket to stay warm. Renwe and Staufo continued to consume the jerky at a faster rate than Jean had planned on, so she warned them that they may have to cut back on their jerky consumption—they had a long way to go before they would arrive at Bent's Fort.

It was easy to construct a temporary corral every evening for their animals. They knew that there were a lot of horse thieves out there, so they tried to remain vigilant—even when there were no signs of other travelers along the trail. Then, one morning, as they were saddling up the horses, they realized that one Morgan mare was missing. No one had heard anything unusual the night before, so they had no idea when the theft had occurred. Was it possible that the mare wandered away from the camp during the night? They checked the local area and could not find the missing horse. Were there any wagon trains close by that could have spotted the small group of Cherokees and stole the mare? No. Were there any Indians around? No.

The particular mare that had disappeared was about the most docile they owned. She was also one of the largest animals in the group, so whoever took her picked the cream of the crop. "At least they didn't get the stallion," Howey commented.

Arnest knew that the stallion would be the hardest animal to steal because he would not allow himself to be taken from his 'brood' of nine mares. "I'm surprised that the stallion didn't make a big fuss when one of his mares was led away," Arnest added. "We're probably lucky that no one got shot last night."

For the remainder of the trip the group kept one horse fully saddled when night-time came. The animal remained at the campfire, ready to ride if another horse-theft was discovered.

❦   ❦   ❦

Two days later, when Howey was in the lead, he spotted a group of three men who were rendering a large animal just off the trail. As the Cherokees got closer they realized that the animal was a bison, and the hunters were skinning the carcass. One of the men was also in the process of cutting a hind-hock free from the carcass, and when he finished the job he put the hock into a buck-board wagon close by. The Cherokees passed by without making any move toward the hunters, and not long after they passed by, the hunters finished their rendering and drove the buckboard north, away from the trail. Staufo and Renwe both wanted to return to the dead animal and cut off more of the meat, but Arnest stopped them cold. "You're not going back to that dead bison," Arnest declared. "There may be Plains Indians in the area, and if they spot us close to the carcass then we may be given the blame for shooting the animal. I don't know what the rules are out here, but I don't want to have to fight a bunch of Plains Indians over a bison carcass."

Then Arnest added, "Staufo and Renwe, you will have your chance to shoot a bison later. We don't need the meat now and we don't need to fight a war with the Plains Indians. Just keep on riding!"

Two days later, when they camped close to a wagon train that had signs on the wagons proclaiming them as emigrants from Illinois, the wagonmaster told them that the U. S. Cavalry had found three dead hunters at a water well just north of the trail. "Whatever those hunters did," he commented, "caused the Indians to get pretty angry, because the Troopers said they had 50 arrows in them."

Arnest and Jean made sure that Renwe and Staufo heard that comment by the wagonmaster.

CHAPTER 3

Fort Bent

The Simmons arrived at Bent's Fort twenty-five days after they left their farm in the Cherokee Nation Territory. The fort was the most impressive building they had seen since they began their travels (other than the stores in Dodge City). It was one-story high at some places and two-stories high at others. The outside surface of the fort was covered in stucco. There was a large livery stable at one corner of the fort, a bivouac area for a platoon of cavalry soldiers, a place for people to 'bunk' amidst a large quantity of dry hay, a small saloon, a general store, and places in the center court where passers-through could tie their animals and view all the trinkets and gear that the local populace displayed for prospective customers. The local populace was a mix of Mexicans, Plains Indians, multi-ethnic fur trappers, and a few eastern white families that had made the trek from eastern Missouri to start life all over again. Spanish was the dominant language.

One notable difference between Fort Bent and Dodge City was the lack of firearms at Fort Bent—these people were farmers, not gun-slingers. They valued horses as a means of travel, but the types of horses that they valued most were the ones that could pull a plow.

The fur trappers were predominantly French-speaking. They spent very little time at the fort—they presented their pelts to a buyer inside the general store, haggled over the price, were paid in cash, and departed the premises after consuming a few shots of whiskey at the saloon.

It was at one of these 'trinkets' places in the center of the fort (a large blanket laid out on the hot summer turf by an old Indian) that Howey found a pair of binoculars that struck his fancy. He paid for the binoculars, and then raised the issue of whether or not the equipment was stolen from the U. S. Army (since it had the words 'U. S. Army' engraved into one side of the binoculars). The sales person assured Howey that these binoculars were taken from a dead Apache warrior in the Dakota Territory and they were no longer a part of the Army inventory. It didn't make a lot of sense, but Howey bought the binoculars and used them the rest of the trip.

At the U. S. Government Land office, which adjoined the fort, the Cherokees found that most of the land around the fort had long-since been deeded away to emigrants from the East. There was some available land south of the fort, on a high plateau, but it had no access to Arkansas River water. The agent at the Land Office explained that the land was more suitable for 'ranchers' than it was for 'farmers'. He suggested that there was some land for sale 100 miles to the east, right along the Arkansas River, near a settlement called 'Pueblo', but the price was high (over $5 an acre). The Simmons knew that this story was not entirely true because they had passed through Pueblo a few days earlier and found no land for sale.

The group decided to rest for a couple of days at Bent's Fort, so they spent the daylight hours talking to local people about what farming land was available along the river. Most of the locals gave the same advice: Go north (away from the Arkansas River) and head for the south fork of the South Platte River. There you will find land for sale along the South Platte that is reasonably priced. The land along the Arkansas River was more fertile, but it also cost a lot more money. Arnest bought a crude map of the land running north and south along the foothills of the Rocky Mountains—it showed the locations of several forts along the South Platte, with names like 'Fort Lupton', 'Trapper's Fort', 'Fort Vasquez', and 'Fort St. Vrain'.

"You will find a lot of farmers along the South Platte River just as the river breaks out of the Rocky Mountains," one soldier told them. "But fifty miles east of the river the land becomes bone-dry. So don't waste your time out on the prairie, way east of the mountains."

One of the locals also told the Simmons that it might be better if they started north soon, because old Mr. Bent was in the middle of a continuing argument with the U. S. Cavalry about keeping the cavalrymen and horses in his fort for a small amount of money. Bent was threatening to burn down the fort. "Sometimes Old Man Bent does crazy things," one settler explained. "It may be a good idea to steer clear of the fort for now. Bent has already built a new fort about a hundred miles north of here—it is named 'Fort St. Vrain', and it is supposed to be in the new center of the beaver trapping empire. He may burn this fort down just to spite the U. S. Cavalry—he's that kind of a person."

The next day the group headed north for the South Platte River. To get there they had to go up a series of 'steppes' that brought the Simmons closer to the mountains and to a higher elevation each time. All around them there were small streams flowing south that formed the headwaters of the Arkansas River. Then the small streams stopped and they passed over a dry plateau that separated the Arkansas River from the South Platte River. A day later the Cherokees knew when they were close to the South Platte because the air had a sweet, moist smell again. They passed two small villages of Plains Indians and traded wide-brim, woven Cherokee 'cavalry' hats for small quantities of smoked bison and deer meat. They had been warned never to ride directly into the center of a Plains Indian village—strangers were expected to remain on the periphery unless they were invited to approach the center of the village by a personal invitation from the Chief. All bartering occurred on the periphery, usually conducted by young braves who had acquired English or Mexican language skills.

There was no time to hunt for large animals, and even if they shot one, they would be forced to leave most of the meat behind. Staufo was still itching to kill a bison. The best shot in the group was Renwe, and he managed to kill fresh meat about every third or fourth day. Whatever he killed had to be cooked and eaten immediately. The oils in the jackrabbit or prairie dog meat kept their alimentary tracts well lubricated, but Jean kept her 'ace in the hole' to service anyone who became constipated—dried apricots. Their jerky supply was running low, and would have to be re-supplied in the next week. Renwe and Staufo continued to over-graze the jerky in their saddlebags, so Arnest,

Jean, and Howey cut back on their daily noon-meal staple to make sure the boys didn't run out.

Once the South Fork of the Platte River burst-out of the Rocky Mountains, it made a sweeping left-turn and proceeded due north, paralleling the front range for about 70 miles. Then it made a huge swing to the east-northeast. It meandered along for over 200 miles before it joined the North Platte River, and then the combined waters of the North Platte and the South Platte flowed due east to the Missouri River.

The Simmons decided to look for farmland in the first 70 miles of the South Platte, where it crossed lush fields of cattle feed and fruit trees. Since there were forts about every ten miles of so, security and protection from the Plains Indians seemed not to be a problem.

CHAPTER 4

Fort Lupton

This was the time of year when the rivers that flow out of the Rocky Mountains look their very best. The snowmelt had begun a month earlier in the high altitude crevices and crannies of the Rocky Mountains, and now the collected waters were pouring out onto the plains to the east (which was considered to be good farm land) or to the west (which was largely uncharted and had the reputation of being unfarmable. This was not true of course, but this is what the farmers believed).

Flooding was a real problem at this time of year, but by late August (just two months from now) the South Platte would be reduced to a slowly meandering stream that one could cross with ease (you got wet up to your knees, and maybe up to your rump if you stepped in a hole). By late September the stream would be reduced to a trickle, and the source of all the water (the crevices and crannies of the Rocky Mountains) would already be collecting new snows and ice for the next year's runoff.

Irrigation was the answer to the inconsistent water supply on the plains east of the Rockies, and everybody knew it.

Fort Lupton was situated on a sandbar about two hundreds yards east of the South Platte River. It was all adobe. It had been built by Lt. Lancaster P. Lupton, a West Point graduate who had resigned his Army commission in 1836 to conduct trade with the Plains Indians and the fur trappers. After twelve years of trading in a steadily-dwindling beaver-pelt and bison-hide market, Lupton gave up and moved away to raise cattle on a large spread to the south. Twenty years later his family made its mark as fur traders on the eastern edge of the Sierra Nevada Mountains, close to a village later named 'Reno'. The new owners of Fort Lupton were suffering great financial setbacks, and the handful of families who lived close to the fort in rough pine-slab cabins knew that the fort's demise was imminent. Without the pelt and hide trade, no one there could make a living. By this time most of the fur and hide trading had moved farther north along the South Platte River, to Fort St. Vrain (which was owned by Mr. Bent).

The Cherokees set up camp on a secluded sandbar south of Fort Lupton, and Arnest sought-out the owner of the land to ask for permission to camp there. Most of the land close to the river was already fenced, but this particular sandbar was not. The neighbors told Arnest that the man who owned the big bend in the river was an Easterner and he never came to the Kansas Territory to view his land. They also told Arnest that he wasn't the first person to camp on that site.

Just to the north of the fort there were workmen digging an east-west canal to take the river water farther onto the farmland, which was mostly flat.

The Cherokee group spent several days scouting the area in the vicinity of Fort Lupton, with mixed results. It was generally conceded that the beaver pelt and bison hide business was all moving north to Fort St. Vrain, 14 miles downstream. But this movement might be to the advantage of the Simmons, who were looking for inexpensive farmland. If the Fort Lupton area people moved away, the land would decrease in price. Unfortunately, to this point, they found no farmers who were anxious to sell their land along the South Platte.

When Howey began checking the animals' hooves (since they had traveled almost 900 miles, and the animals were used to a plush life at the old homestead) he found severe degradation of their hooves and iron shoes. Four of the animals definitely needed to be reshod immediately. Since the group had been in and out of Fort Lupton several times, they knew that there was a blacksmith inside the fort, close to the main entrance. The smoke and the heat from the forge filled the fort when the winds were coming from the south.

Arnest and Staufo led the horses to the forge while Howey and Renwe were out hunting for the evening meal. The forge was busy, and a dozen U. S. Cavalry horses were moving nervously inside the blacksmith's corral, trying to find a way out of the compound. The blacksmith was young, probably less than twenty years old, with black hair and the beginnings of a black beard. His skin was dark brown, but as soon as he took off his huge fireproof gloves, his hands and lower arms were milky-white in color. He was missing two front teeth, but that was not unusual for men in his age group.

"What do you need, Mister?" the blacksmith asked Arnest. Arnest explained that their horses had come all the way from the Cherokee Nation Territory and they needed to be reshod. They also needed some kind of treatment for the cracks in their hooves. The blacksmith lifted the front hoof of the nearest animal and examined it closely. "I hope you ain't planning to return east any time real soon," he suggested. "This animal needs new shoes and ointment for cracked hooves. You better plan to keep her out on the sandbar or some place that's soft and cool for at least a month so her hooves can heal."

The Cherokees nodded their heads in agreement. The blacksmith looked at the other three hooves of the mare, and then did the same thing for the other three mares. "These sure are fine lookin' animals," he told Staufo. "These may be the only Morgan horses for a hundred miles around!"

Arnest and the blacksmith haggled a little about the price to treat the horses, but one thing was for sure—the treatments had to be done, and the quicker the better. 'How quickly can you reshoe these animals?" Arnest asked.

The blacksmith thought for a few moments, and then replied "Give me two days to finish up these Cavalry mounts, and I can get your animals reshod on the third day. That be Friday, as I remember." Arnest told the blacksmith that they had five other horses that were in better shape hoof-wise than these four mares, but they might need some attention also.

"Then bring all the animals here, early Friday morning," the blacksmith suggested. "I need an early start."

"What is early?" Staufo asked.

"Be here about an hour after sunup," the blacksmith suggested, "and I should be able to work on all your horses that day." Then he added, "Are they all Morgan horses?"

"Yes sir, they are" Arnest replied.

The blacksmith turned his head in disbelief. "We haven't seen the likes of that many Morgan horses in this county in years," he said. "I tell you right now, Mister, that you better watch these animals day and night until you go back East. We got some mean people around here that would almost kill for horse-flesh like this."

Arnest nodded in agreement. As they were about to leave, Staufo approached the blacksmith and offered his right hand. "I'm Staufo Simmons," he told the blacksmith. "We come from Tahlequah, in the Cherokee Nation."

The blacksmith shook Staufo's hand and turned to Arnest. "My name is Tim Wisnant," he said. "We live just a few hundred yards south of here, on the river."

"We been here over twenty years", he added. "Twenty years too long!"

"I'm Arnest Simmons," Arnest replied.

There was a pause, and then Tim shook his head up and down. "Tahlequah", he repeated. "Then you be Cherokee Indians."

"Yes, we are," Arnest answered.

"We used to have a full-blooded Cherokee right here at the fort," Tim began. "Then one day last month he come by and says to me, 'I'm goin' to California and gonna get rich.' I knew what he was talking about—we hear about gold in California all the time. I should have gone with him."

Then Tim continued with, "My father says that all this talk about gold is pure foolishness—there's some people in California that want to sell property there and they keep comin' up with the wild gold stories."

"Have you ever mined for gold?" Arnest asked Tim.

"No Sir, can't say as I have," was the reply. "You ever mined for gold?"

Arnest laughed, and then told Tim about their gold-hunting days over twenty years ago. "We went to a place in Georgia named 'Licklog' and filed a claim. We worked the claim for over two years, and made a little money. But when it was all over we had to come back to our farm again, and plant again, just like we did every other year."

Staufo added something to the story: "But the family group who went to Licklog also brought back a Morgan stallion and that's the reason all five of us ride in style!"

"Yes Sir, that's riding in style," Tim commented.

"One thing I remember about that Cherokee," Tim said. "He never had to shave—he had the smoothest face I have ever seen. He had real high cheekbones that made him look fierce, but he was really a gentle person. He didn't have a lot of wrinkles, either."

"Do you have to shave?" Tim asked Arnest.

"Never shaved a day in my life," Arnest answered.

"But I can grow hair on the top of my head, for which I am very thankful," Arnest added. "Hair on top of your head keeps your brains from frying in the sun."

As Arnest and Staufo were leaving the forge, Tim called out to them, "If you decide to go gold-hunting to California, just let me know. I wanta go with you."

"What makes you so sure that there really is a big gold strike in California?" Arnest asked Tim.

"Everybody who comes through here is talking about the gold," Tim responded.

"Are these people going west to find gold, or are they coming from the west with gold in their saddlebags?" Arnest asked.

Tim had to think about this question for a minute or two. "I guess it's mostly Easterners from places like St Louis or Kansas City who are in a big rush to get to California before all the gold is mined-out," he explained.

Then Tim added, "Talk to the man who runs the general store in the fort. He has a newspaper from Kansas City that his brother sent to him last month, and the paper tells what's going on in California. But you gotta be able to read."

Arnest was glad that he knew how to read.

Staufo and Arnest waved goodbye and led their horses back to the campsite on the river. Everywhere they went the next two days, people were talking about the gold discovery in California—maybe this was a *real* gold strike this time.

On Friday, Tim Wisnant checked all the horses for shoe wear and cracks in their hooves. He had a salve named 'Venice Turpentine' that he mail-ordered from St. Louis, and he put the salve in all the cuts and breaks in the animal's hooves. He gave Arnest two cans of the salve, telling him that he may need the ointment for the return trip home.

While Tim and Arnest were talking, an older man walked into the forge. Tim introduced him to Arnest and Staufo as his father, Henry Wisnant. The old man walked rather stiffly, and he dragged his right leg a little. He told Arnest that he had been thrown from a horse a month ago, and he was recuperating very slowly. "My son tells me that you're going to need a place to camp for the next month, so why don't you camp over close to our place? There's some high ground near the river that stays dry when the river rises—the place you are camped at right now goes underwater from time to time."

Arnest thanked him for the offer, and said that he would like to move to this new campsite because one other person at the fort also told him that the river sometimes floods their present campsite location. "Do you mind if we move tonight?" Arnest asked.

"That will be fine," was Henry's answer.

Arnest decided that this might be a good time to ask the old man about land that was for sale around Fort Lupton, so he asked him: "Any body around here wanting to sell their land?"

Henry though a minute, then answered in the negative. "There's some land for sale away from the river," Henry added, "and the new buyer would have irrigation water rights. There are two east-west canals being dug to irrigate land on either side of the river. But you're better off to own the land right on the river—that way you know you will always have water for your crops.

Agreed.

After Henry left, Tim mentioned that their land (the Wisnant land) probably *was* for sale because neither his father nor he ever intended to be a farmer. They owned a forge so they could stay away from farming. "The farmers on the river ask a lot of money for their land when they decide to sell it—usually $3.00 an acre," Tim explained. "If Henry decided to sell he would ask $1,900 for the whole 640 acre section. Nobody around here has $1,900.00."

"Do farmers share-crop around here?" Arnest asked.

"What does that mean?" Tim returned.

Arnest explained: "The person who wants the land plants the crops and harvests the crops, then he and the owner of the land split the profits every year. After ten or twelve years the man who has been planting the acreage pays the old owner some small amount of money and the farm is deeded to him."

"Never heard of that before," Tim said. "I couldn't imagine my father doing something like that. But I will tell you that if someone came along with the $1,900.00 to buy our whole section, my father would sell in a minute and move to some big town like Kansas City where he could lay brick or stone. He really likes to put in new fireplaces."

Before Arnest and Staufo left the fort with their horses, Arnest walked over to the general store to see if there really was a Kansas City newspaper that explained what was going on in California. The front page of the newspaper was nailed to the wall behind the counter and the owner offered to read it to Arnest. The article said there was a huge gold find at a place east of Sacramento City, California, at a place called 'Sutter's Mill'. The story also explained that the gold was located on government land, and anyone could come there and file a claim to mine for the gold.

"No wonder gold fever is catching on so fast," Arnest thought to himself.

The next day Arnest made Henry Wisnant an offer to sell his land by share-cropping and a one-time cash settlement twelve years from now, but Henry refused the offer. He wanted the section of land to be totally his or totally somebody else's, but he didn't want any land-sharing.

So that was the end of that.

One evening Tim came over to the Simmons campsite and he, Renwe, and Staufo swapped stories for several hours about farm life, camping life, and life in the wild, wild west. Tim told them that there hadn't been an Indian uprising in this part of the Kansas Territory in 20 years, but that could change in a hurry. "For one thing," Tim mentioned, "the U. S. Government keeps trying to force the Indians into a smaller and smaller space, and the Indians can still remember when all this land belonged to them."

"If I was an Indian," Tim continued, "I would fight like hell to keep the U. S. Government from doing what they're trying to do to the Indians right now."

Arnest, Jean, and Howey knew something about being forced into a smaller and smaller space. They also knew that the government never stopped nagging at you until you did what the white man wanted.

A week later Tim showed the Cherokees a map cut into a piece of rawhide that claimed to be a map to the gold fields of California. The map started at Fort Laramie, a hundred miles north of Fort Lupton, and ended in central California at 'Sutter's Mill', near a town named 'Coloma'.

"Where did you get the map?" Renwe asked.

"You remember that bunch of U. S. Cavalry horses that I reshod a week and a half ago?" Tim answered. "Well, the Sergeant that owns those horses gave me this map when he picked up his horses. He said he wasn't going to be able to use the map 'cause his enlistment wasn't up for another two years. He didn't want to desert the Army just to pan for gold—the U. S. Army hangs deserters around here."

Tim continued: "His detachment bunks at Fort St Vrain, and they lost their blacksmith up there to typhoid fever or something like that. So he had to bring his horses down here to re-shoe, and I did it for him all in one day. To show his appreciation, he gave me the map."

Everyone looked at the map. There were some distances shown on the map, but other sections only had small squares with names printed next to them, like 'Last Chance Well' or 'Humboldt Sinkhole'. The Great Salt Lake was shown at the very center of the map.

"Is it really 900 miles to the California gold fields?" Staufo asked.

"There's no way to tell from this map," Tim responded. "Notice that there's no distance shown between the eastern start of the Humboldt River and the end of the river close to the Sierra Nevada Mountains. Maybe the map-maker forgot to measure the distance—he would have needed the world's longest piece of string to do that."

Everyone laughed. "How long does it take to get to the gold fields?" Howey asked.

Tim had an answer for that question: "According to the words at the bottom of the map, any fool can get to the gold fields in an oxen-drawn conestoga wagon in 120 days, and if you travel light using horses, you can get there in 75 to 90 days."

Since the Cherokees had come from the Cherokee Nation Territory to Fort Lupton, a distance of close to 900 miles in forty days, taking 120 days to travel another 900 miles didn't seem to be all that difficult. One thing was for sure though—the 900 miles farther west passed through some gawd-awful deserts and mountains that human beings were never meant to pass through.

"I wonder how people get through all that terrible country," Jean commented. "If you go in the summer you burn up, and if you go in the winter you freeze."

Tim answered with, "You go between the summer and the winter, and that way you burn less and freeze less. There's a guy at the fort who says he has been to California twice, and it might be good to talk to him about how a wagon train or horse team gets to California all in one piece."

"What's his name?" Howey asked.

"Bixby" was the answer.

"What's his first name?" Howey asked.

"I don't think he has a first name," Tim replied. "Everybody just calls him 'Bixby.'"

"Where do we go to talk to him?" Arnest asked.

"I'll find out where he is," Tim responded. "He has a favorite watering hole just outside the main gate of the fort, and I'll tell the saloon keeper that I need to talk to Bixby. He'll find him."

Renwe and Staufo were really excited now! This was the first time that their father had admitted having any interest in another gold hunt. They knew that their mother would be highly skeptical about traveling another 900 miles west—the South Platte River was as far west as she wanted to go. Still, if Arnest was interested in another gold hunt, maybe Jean was also. After all, Jean was the real decision-maker in their family—if she agreed to do something then they did it. Once the decision was made, Arnest just tended to the details. Howey was easy—he did whatever the main group wanted to do.

Howey's problem was that he was always ready to jump into the middle of something new, and he had gotten burned a couple of times. Like the time he bought fifty old Cavalry mounts to re-sell, then found out that every one of them had been ridden so hard and so long by overweight cavalrymen that there wasn't any life left in them. Some cavalry units went through an entire issue of new horses in a year or two. From Jean's viewpoint, Howey had refused to grow up. She was surprised that Claire had put up with him over the years. Still, Howey was a good husband and he worked very hard to make life pleasant for Claire. They were both disappointed that they never had any children, but they were past the child-bearing years now. There was no looking back at life at this time.

That night Jean and Arnest talked for a long time in their tiny, white tent. Arnest wanted to know how Jean felt about this possible California adventure, and Jean wanted to know how deeply Arnest was committed to doing such a thing. She knew that Renwe, Staufo, and Howey would choose to continue on to California at the drop of a hat. But this wasn't a democracy. There would be no trip west without the consent of both Arnest and Jean. They both knew that.

"We'll talk some more later," Arnest suggested as they fell off to sleep.

CHAPTER 5

Bixby

Tim found a reason to stop by the Cherokee campsite nearly every evening now, and he always wanted to talk about the same thing—going to California. He brought the Venice Turpentine ointment for the horses' hooves, and applied it while he talked with Renwe and Staufo. He would leave just as the sun was going down. "Those animals are looking better every day," he would always say. One evening he mentioned that Mr. Bent had had a first-class fight with the U. S. Cavalry at Fort Bent and he burned down the fort. "Must be hard to do business with that man," Tim commented.

Then, one evening, Tim approached the campsite with more enthusiasm than usual, and everyone knew that something good had happened. "I saw Bixby today," Tim announced. "He is ready to talk about California if you all are ready to listen."

Yes, everyone was ready to listen.

"I'll bring him here to your campsite tomorrow evening," Tim suggested. "We need some time to talk, so I better get him here at least an hour before sunset."

Yes, that would be an excellent time. If Tim was excited, then the Cherokees ought to be excited also.

The next evening, right after the evening meal, the group saw two men walking toward them, coming from the fort. One was a lot shorter than the other. The tall man was Tim, so the short man had to be 'Bixby'. When the two approached the campfire, Tim introduced 'Elias Bixby' to everyone present.

Bixby was an older man, probably a few years older than Howey, and he was a little stooped-over. Even in the fading light of sunset they could see that he was very dark—sunburned is the word. He had the usual stubby beard that had been black at one time but was now a mixture of gray and white. He also had a small mustache, which was unusual because caring for a mustache on the prairie is a real chore. Beards just grow, but mustaches have to be tended to—else the mustache covers up your mouth and you find it harder and harder to feed yourself.

The Simmons always had a problem offering a visitor in their home some liquid refreshment because they shunned alcoholic beverage and they just plain didn't like the taste of coffee. At the farm they always had some kind of juice available, and in some of the juices they placed 'bitters' so the drink had a little more 'body' to it—more of an 'adult' taste. Jean and Arnest knew that they should have shed their personal preferences a long time ago and learned to drink black coffee, but the stuff was so awful that they just couldn't stomach it.

In this case Bixby had brought his own refreshments—a bottle of whiskey. Tim was a little embarrassed by the presence of the alcohol, but there was nothing he could do about it. When Tim got to know Jean and Arnest better, he wondered why the two hadn't joined the Mormon Church. "You all certainly have the temperament for the 'Church of Latter Day Saints'" he commented.

After the introductions, Tim asked Bixby to tell them what he knew about traveling to California. As it turned out, Bixby knew a great deal about the subject, and he kept them there by the campfire for two hours. Even when the mosquitoes moved in and started biting hard, there were more questions by the Cherokees and more answers by Bixby.

Finally, after Howey had been bitten most ferociously by a world-class mosquito, he asked that they continue the discussion the next day, at a time slightly before the evening meal, when the sun was still showing its face in the western sky. Jean immediately invited Bixby too come over to the campsite early the next evening, and they would have the evening meal shortly thereafter. Bixby promised to return.

Arnest had a theory about mosquito bites—you wouldn't feel the bites if you never scratched the bite the first time. Jean was pretty well covered-up with thick cloth when the mosquitoes invaded, but Arnest left himself open as fair game with bare arms and shoulders. When everyone went to sleep, Jean immediately brought out a small bottle of liniment that she kept in her saddlebag, and she carefully doused each of his offending bug bites. The liniment was yellow-looking and it smelled terrible, but it seemed to help the constant itch of the mosquito bites. There was definitely some sulfur in the mixture.

"This liniment comes from an apothecary in Joplin," Jean told Arnest. "It says right here on the bottle that it will relieve the itch of mosquito bites instantly—or your money back."

Arnest looked at his arms and felt the back of his neck. "When we get back to Joplin I want to talk to the owner of that apothecary," he said. "I think we want our money back."

Having done her bit to help Arnest, she immediately went off to sleep. But Arnest was not cured of the itch, and he spent the next two hours trying to find a position where the horse blanket that they had thrown over themselves did not excite the mosquito bites over and over. No such luck.

The next evening, which happened to be the Fourth of July, when Bixby returned to the Cherokee campfire, the questions the Simmons wanted to ask were a little more organized. When asked how quickly they must depart to beat the winter snows in the Sierra Nevadas, Bixby quoted the old adage that a wagon party had to clear Fort Bridger by the end of July to ensure safe passage all the way to California. This gave a wagon train time to get through the Truckee Pass or the Carson Pass by the fifteen of October. "We're just three weeks from the end of July," Bixby reminded them.

Then Staufo asked Bixby if the Donner Party of 1846—1847 fame had made it through the Truckee Pass by that date. Bixby replied with, "No, they began the march through the Truckee Pass almost two weeks later."

The first question that Arnest asked was about the condition of the Morgan horses—were they in good enough condition for another long trip? Tim answered that the Morgan's hooves had healed significantly, and they were as ready to travel as they would ever be.

The next question was about their financial condition—did they have enough money to return home? Howey answered, "Yes." Did they have enough money to go to California? Howey said he didn't know what the answer was—but they had money to last for at least the next three months. It would be foolish to spend all their money because, if they found land for sale, they wouldn't have any money left to buy it.

What about food? Jean replied that there was plenty of jerky and bacon and flour for biscuits. They had re-supplied all these items at Bent Fort. But they presently carried no food for the horses—the group counted on always finding grass for forage along the trail. Was this true if the group went west? Bixby had a lot to say about this question. He told them that both horses and mules could forage off the land all the way to Salt Lake City and about 100 miles west of the Great Salt Lake. Then the forage would decrease significantly, as would the fresh water, until they reached a group of small water wells between the Salt Lake desert and the start of the Humboldt River. These were wells that held water most of the time, but they could also go dry. Grass and other forage was a big problem on this part of the trek to California, but the biggest problem was the lack of good water.

Bixby also mentioned that the Humboldt River was a 'fresh water' river in name only—the Humboldt River began at a 'nothing' place in the Utah Territory and ended in an equally 'nothing' place in the Nevada Territory. As you moved farther west, the water in the Humboldt became more and more nasty. But the animals would drink it no matter how bad it got.

The eastern end of the Humboldt River was fed by two small rivers from the northeast, but the rivers existed above ground only at selected times of year. When the rivers moved underground the Humboldt seemed to spring out of the middle of nowhere.

He also explained that neither horses nor mules knew anything about conserving water—if you offered them a full bucket of water they would either drink it all or slop it around to cool themselves off. To conserve water, Bixby always gave each of his animals water separately, in a canvas bag that the animal had to dip its head into to reach the water at the bottom. The animal always drank all the water in the canvas bag, but they didn't waste any of it.

Human beings had to obey the water conservation rules also. Bixby explained that all the water wells along the California Trail between Salt Lake City and the Sierra Nevada had been dug by Mormon soldiers. At each well there was a sign asking the emigrants to dig the wells a little bit deeper, but there was never anyone at the wells to make sure that you did your part in digging the well.

There were no signs anywhere along the trek that pointed the travelers toward California—the leader of each group was supposed to know when to turn and when to go straight. There were a few poisoned water wells along the way, but they could always be spotted by the number of dead animal carcasses at the site.

Jean asked how many days it took to go from Fort Lupton to the Sutter Mill. Bixby answered that it would take 70 days at a minimum, and 90 days at worst. It would be best if they cleared the Sierra Nevadas by the end of September. The question arose: "If this was a 900 mile trip, why would it take 90 days to get there?" Bixby answered that there were good days where they would make 20 miles easily, but there were also bad days where they would be lucky to cover 5 miles. If they encountered significant snow in the Sierra Nevadas, this would slow them down a lot. But the 'desert' problem was an 800 mile problem—the 'snow' problem was a 50 mile problem at this time of year. In February and March the entire 'central basin' from Salt Lake City to the Sierras was covered in snow, sometimes up to twenty feet deep. No one crossed this stretch of desert in the winter.

"Would there be trouble with the Plains Indians?" Howey asked. Bixby answered: "We may see some Indians as much as 100 miles west of Salt Lake City, but they know that the trek becomes very bad very quickly, and they stay away from the Humboldt River. The next time you confront a significant number of Indians is when you begin the climb through the Truckee Pass to cross the Sierra Nevadas. Once you clear the Sierra Nevadas you find a whole new group of Indians who make California their home."

"How cold would it be in the Sierra Nevadas in September or October?" Arnest asked. Answer: "As soon as the sun goes down the temperature goes below freezing. When you reach the valley where Sutter's Mill is located the temperature goes up in a hurry. But in the dead of winter there is snow at Sutter's Mill and below freezing temperatures."

"Do we need special gear for the horses for cold weather?"

Answer: "To be absolutely safe, you should have some kind of covering for the animal's legs in extremely cold weather. But we should clear the Sierra Nevadas before this extreme cold occurs." Staufo couldn't resist this response: "You mean like the extreme weather that the Donner Wagon Train experienced at this same pass two years ago?"

"Yes," was the reply.

"Does it ever rain in California?" Staufo asked. Answer: "The rainy season is September through February. The rest of the time it stays pretty dry."

The group of Cherokees was amazed at how much Bixby seemed to know about the far West. He was a walking encyclopedia. "How do you know all these things?" Renew asked. Answer: "These are the same questions that people ask every time they begin crossing the land between Salt Lake City and San Francisco."

Bixby had only entered California twice in his life, but he had participated in treks from Salt Lake City to the Sierra Nevadas four other times because wagon train leaders needed experienced scouts to stay in front of the main party and look for trouble. Once the wagon train reached the Sierra Nevadas there was no need for scouts, so he was paid by the wagon train leader and returned to Salt Lake City, Fort Bridger, and Fort Laramie. Most wagon trains paid a group of Paiute Indians to lead them across the Sierra Nevadas.

Are there better ways to get to California? Staufo asked. Bixby answered: "There are three main ways to get to California by land. One way is through a south opening in the mountains southwest of Santa Fe, crossing a stretch of 200 miles of desert on the way to Los Angeles. The second way is through the

Truckee Pass or Carson Pass, and they are only forty miles apart. This is the 'central' route. The third way is through Oregon, the 'northern' route."

Next question: "Why was he willing to go to California at this time?"

Bixby had an immediate answer: "It's all about the gold, son, it's all about the gold!

Arnest asked if there were more questions, and there were none. Then he asked if anyone wanted to speak to the group and voice his/her views. Again, no one responded. So Arnest told the Cherokees that they would now vote on what they would do. Arnest told them: "If you want to go to California then hold your right hand out in front of you. If you want to return home, then hold your left hand out in front of you."

The Simmons boys immediately held their right hand out, as did Howey. Arnest made no move, but looked over at Jean. In a few seconds she held out her right hand also. Now it was safe for Arnest to hold out his right hand and announce that the group would depart for California in two days.

Tim instinctively held his right hand out also. "I'm in this adventure too" he said.

"You can count me in," Bixby told the group. So the trip was set.

Jean was worried that Tim's folks would become angry when they heard that Tim was going with them to California. Maybe they counted on him to operate the forge. So she walked over to the Wisnant cabin and spoke with Henry and his wife about Tim. The Wisants offered no resistance to his making the trip—they knew he was anxious to get away from Fort Lupton and the home-town forge.

CHAPTER 6

West to California

The first thing Tim did the next day was to look over the herd of horses that the Wisnants offered for sale at their farm. He picked out two paint horses, one stallion and one mare. He liked the idea of swapping the horses every day so each horse had a hard day (with a rider) followed by an easy day (no rider).

Tim had a rifle of his own, and he knew how to fire it. It was an 1804, .60 caliber flintlock. He bought a sidearm from one of the neighbors, a percussion two-shot derringer. His mother gave him an ample supply of jerky, flour, smoked bacon, and dried persimmons that she grew in her own backyard. Tim had received another shipment of Venice Turpentine ointment for the horses from St. Louis, and most of the shipment ended up in his saddlebags.

Jean wrote a short letter to Claire, and told her that the group was going to the California gold fields. They would return in about 18 months. If Claire had to write to them, she should do so by addressing a letter to Arnest Simmons at Salt Lake City General Delivery in the Utah Territory or the Sutter Mill General Delivery in the California Territory. If that didn't work, send mail to the San Francisco Post Office.

Howey also wrote a short letter to his wife, and slipped it in the envelope with Jean's letter. This was a hard thing for Howey to do because he could write so few words in English or in the Cherokee language.

Henry gave Tim some blacksmithing tools that were small and lightweight. "You never know when you're going to have to ply your trade out in the middle of some desert," he told Tim.

The Simmons had enough cooking utensils so Tim left his at home. His folks presented him with a broad-brimmed felt hat that would keep the hot sun off his face and neck. "Tim sunburns pretty easy," his mother told Jean. The Wisnants also gave each person in the Cherokee party a large, red bandana. They were concerned about the scorching heat of the desert in August and September.

Arnest replaced the one Morgan mare that had been stolen with a sorrel mare from Henry Wisnant's collection of horses for sale.

Bixby always traveled with four mules. He was concerned that none of the Cherokees had provided for adequate water bags, so he went to the fort and arranged for a local leather-works seamstress to make 16 of them—one to be placed on each horse and each mule. The lady knew how to make waterproof bags—she sewed a first seam, and then stuffed wool into the seam just before she sewed the second seam. Making the waterbags took a day longer than Bixby planned, so the trip was delayed one day.

On July 8, 1849, about an hour before sunup, the group began the trek to California. Bixby had a detailed map of the land between Fort Lupton and Fort Bridger. The could go almost due north to the Nebraska Territory and Fort Laramie, then turn west through the South Pass of western Nebraska, and then turn southwest to Bridger and the Great Salt Lake. This was a well-used route and there was always 'safety in numbers' when the white man crossed the plains. Or, they could skirt along the edge of the Rocky Mountains using the streambed of the Cache La Poudre River and cut off almost one hundred miles of the trek. The Poudre River provided water all the way to the continental divide, and the pass through the mountains was gentle and predictable. But they would be traveling alone most of the time until they reached Fort Bridger.

Bixby decided that the shortcut was worth the risk, and they headed for the Poudre River. They spent their first night in the Poudre Canyon, on a sandbar at one of the sharp turns in the river. The walls of the canyon were only about sixty feet high, but they were too high to climb if anything went wrong. Bixby explained that the Poudre River was a quiet river—it had no history of flooding.

It took the Cherokee party three days to reach the continental divide. The descent on the western side of the divide was gentle and well-marked by buffalo dung on and beside the trail. There was also the familiar 'cuts' in the trail made by heavy wagons. They reached a 'hollow' in the landscape just past the divide where several small streams made their way north—it was over fifty miles across. The air was fresh and the night was cool. "I wonder why no one lives here," Howey commented.

"There were people living here," Bixby explained. "Then winter came and they all froze to death."

"What about the Indians?" Howey asked.

"You could find them here in the spring and summer, and sometimes into the fall, but they got out before winter came," Bixby answered.

"Where did they go?"

"This valley is ringed by mountains on three sides," Bixby answered. "The only way they could go was north, so that's what they did. They went all the way to the Grand Tetons sometimes, or to the Yellowstone Valley."

❦   ❦   ❦

Renwe saw his first moose late one afternoon, and he wanted to chase the animal and shoot it. But Howey stopped him and promised that he would go hunting with him that evening, after they set-up camp.

That evening they spotted a pronghorn deer, but no moose. Renwe's first shot sailed harmlessly high and to-the-left of the deer at a range of about 200 yards. There wasn't time for a second shot. Renwe and Howey decided that the useful range of the smoothbore flintlock was really only 100 yards or so—at 200 yards the smallest animal you could shoot with certainty would be a bull elephant from Africa who was at least twenty feet high. Shooting game in the West offered a new challenge—there was no easy way to get within 100 yards of the game and remain hidden. This was never a problem in the Cherokee Nation Territory, with its dense undergrowth.

"I wonder how the Indians out here got close enough to shoot an animal with a bow and arrow?" Renwe asked.

"Great patience, great patience, young man," was Bixby's reply. "They had to set-up in a depression in the earth, hope that the wind direction did not change (so man's scent would not drift toward the game) and wait for the animals to come to them."

Renwe and Staufo managed to shoot two prairie dogs. The prairie dog meat was so fatty that you had to eat lots of biscuits to keep the meat down. It didn't help when Bixby reminded them that the prairie dogs that they were eating were high-plains rats.

That evening, about an hour after sunset, they heard the distinctive sound of a large-caliber rifle being discharged. There was no telling where the sound came from, but the group knew that they were not alone any more.

🍁   🍁   🍁

After they crossed the continental divide they aimed for a lesser pass named 'Buffalo Pass' to the southwest. Then they followed another trail to the northwest that was well marked with buffalo dung, but fewer wagon grooves or the marks of horses' hooves. The travelers on this trail must be mostly animals or people who walk—probably Indians.

On the third day after they started the descent from Buffalo Pass they found the remains of a small wagon train spread out across the trail. The group must have been attacked without warning. There were only seven wagons. There were no draft animals in the area and no remains of human beings. "This must have happened at least a year ago," Bixby explained. "Whoever attacked these people, they took everything—all the animals, food, firearms, cooking utensils, water jugs, and the cloth tops off the wagons."

Then he continued with: "Someone came along later and buried the people in the wagon train. This is the far western edge of Comanche territory, and the Comanches never bury their victims."

There was nothing to be done here, so the group of seven continued on their way to Fort Bridger. That night, every time a noise was heard, all seven people sat up in fear, peering into the darkness for any signs of an Indian war party. Bixby tried to comfort them with the words, "No Indian—no Comanche, Sioux, Arapahoe, or what-have-you, fights at night unless they have to. We're safe at night."

That said, the entire group stayed up the entire night anyway, and early the next morning they were anxious to continue on their trek to the west.

According to Bixby, they were about 250 miles from Fort Bridger. They couldn't aim directly northwest for the fort because there were some deep-cut rivers set in canyons in front of them that were not fordable by the group. So they had to continue due west and ford the rivers farther upstream where the rivers were smaller. After several days of moving across plains of buffalo grass, Bixby announced that is was time to turn north and close on Fort Bridger. The trip from Fort Lupton to Fort Bridger took 17 days, so they camped on the outer edge of the fort on July 25. The group exhaled in relief when they arrived since they were now in the midst of hundreds of emigrants just like themselves.

When Bixby visited the fort late that afternoon, he heard that the famous Jim Bridger was somewhere in the fort so he hurried back to the campsite to get Renwe and Staufo. "You gotta come see Jim Bridger," he told them. Renwe and Staufo knew a little about Jim Bridger—there were as many 'yarns' in the west about Bridger as there were about Davy Crockett.

"Did you ever hear the story of Jim Bridger's escape from the Indians in the Yellowstone River?" Bixby asked. He didn't wait for an answer. "The Indians captured Bridger, took his horse, his weapons, and all his clothes, and tied him up to a tree in their camp. During the night he worked his way free and he ran all the way to a French settlement just east of the Grand Tetons—nearly forty miles! The Indians found out that he had escaped and they went after him in the morning. But he got away. Several years later he built this fort so people could have a safe place to stay at night while they were traveling the Mormon Trail or the California Trail."

Compared to the smooth stucco of Bent's Fort on the Arkansas River, this fort was nothing to get excited about. There was a gate on the front, but it didn't look like it was capable of being closed if Indians or some other enemy attacked. Fort Bent was two-stories tall in some areas; Fort Bridger was only one-story tall and the observation towers in the corners were sadly in need of repair. But there was one thing that Bridger had that Bent did not: a huge saloon complete with dancing girls, poker, a forty-foot long bar, and an open invitation to the customers to 'visit with the girls upstairs'. The locals at the fort were doing well, selling all sorts of important items (like ground white flour and corn meal, smoked bacon, and salt) and unimportant items (like a divining rod that would find water for you in the desert).

When Renwe and Staufo indicated that they wanted to go to the saloon and meet Jim Bridger, Arnest decided to go along with them. Howey decided to go also, so only Jean was left at the campsite to guard their animals and belongings.

"We'll be back shortly," Arnest assured her.

To Renwe and Staufo she issued a stern warning, "You leave your sidearms right here at the campfire. I don't want you taking a weapon in that place, you understand?"

The boys nodded and took off their pistol belts. Arnest and Howey had already left their weapons at the campfire. Bixby, however, insisted on carrying his old flintlock double-action derringer. The derringer was a part of his 'uniform', and there was no telling who he would meet at the saloon. "You gotta be prepared to meet your friends," he told Jean.

Bixby was in a hurry. "Come on, come on," he shouted to the boys. "We gotta get there before Bridger decides to leave!"

Jean reminded Arnest that they needed a lot of jerky for the next 500 miles or so, so he should stock-up on the meat at the fort.

So everyone trotted over to the fort, which was only 200 yards away. About two hours later everyone returned to the campsite except Bixby. He had found a couple of old drinking buddies and he told Arnest he would return to the campsite a little later.

"So how was Jim Bridger?" Jean asked the boys when they returned from the fort.

She didn't get an immediate answer, so she asked again. Staufo was less than enthusiastic: "Bixby tells us that this man ran 40 miles to escape his Indian captors—well, the man we saw tonight couldn't run one mile if his life depended on it."

"This is the stuff that legends are made of," Jean thought to herself.

Bixby returned several hours later, smelling like a distillery. But this was the first time he had 'imbibed' in over three weeks, which was probably a record for the old man. He slept soundly after he went into his tent. On some nights Bixby snored terribly, so the group arranged to have his tent set a little farther away from the campfire and a little closer to the animals' corral. Bixby didn't seem to mind—he was used to that.

Jean expected Bixby to be all out of sorts when morning came, but Bixby surprised her by eating a hearty breakfast and sharing a wealth of information that he had gained from his drinking buddies. "They tell me that the Mormon soldiers are working on the trail between Salt Lake City and the Humboldt River," Bixby told the Cherokees. "They also dug the wells in the Salt Lake Desert a lot deeper, so our chances of finding water there are better than usual."

Then he added, "Those wells are always filled with water in the spring, then the water level slowly sinks as summer comes, and by September they go dry again. We should do alright at the wells."

The next day Howey found another pair of binoculars laid out on one of the Indian blankets at the entrance to the fort. This pair was newer than the one he bought at Bent's fort, and it was more powerful. It also had 'U. S. Army' markings all over it. He bought the binoculars and offered the old binoculars to

Bixby, but Bixby declined. "I don't see very well through binoculars," he explained to Howey. "I am basically blind. Thank you for the offer, but no thank you." As time went by the Cherokees realized how poor Bixby's sight really was.

The locals told them they were only 100 miles away from Salt Lake City, but there was a mountain range between Fort Bridger and the Great Salt Lake that would slow them down considerably. The locals also warned that the supply of fresh water was about to end also—once they reached the Great Salt Lake, water would be scarce for almost 600 miles.

Tim made another check of the horses' hooves again, and he was cautiously optimistic about their general health.

They left Fort Bridger before sunrise on July 28. There was no snow in the mountains to the southwest, but the trail was steep, especially after they reached the top of the pass between Fort Bridger and Salt Lake City. The trip down to the city included a series of switchbacks because the mountains were too steep for man or mules or horses, and they would have been totally unmanageable for conestoga wagons without the switchbacks. At two places on the switchbacks they found groups of young soldiers working on the road—part of the Mormon Army commanded by Brigham Young.

CHAPTER 7

The Great Salt Lake

On August 8 the group reached the edges of the Great Salt Lake. As they entered the city limits of Salt Lake City a young man rushed up to them with a map and showed them where the city hall was located. He encouraged them to sign-in at the counter on the first floor of city hall. He explained that the city was constantly receiving letters from back East—family and friends who had lost contact with the emigrants who were going to the Oregon Territory or the California Territory. By signing in at the city hall, these letters of enquiry could be answered.

The young man also mentioned that the Cherokees should send a letter back east telling their families that they had arrived at the Great Salt Lake, because the next post office on the California Trail was 600 miles west—in a place named Monterrey. Jean asked if there was a bank close by, and the young man apologized about the lack of a bank in the Utah Territory. He explained that once their leader, Brigham Young, got the newspaper going and the schools going, his next big task was to build a financial district in downtown Salt Lake City. There were far too many Mormons arriving in Salt Lake City than the city could handle, and the city had run out of farmable land and drinking water. So the Council was sending the new arrivals to points south of the city (as far south as the Mexican border), and as far north as the Canadian border. The purpose of the newspaper was to keep all these people informed about what was going on in the new Mormon empire.

The purpose of the Mormon schools was to teach all the children how to read the newspaper. Jean could understand that idea—it had only been twenty years since the great Cherokee scholar, Sequoyah, had created a written language for the Cherokees, and already most of the children under the age of twelve could read the national Cherokee newspapers, the 'Cherokee Phoenix' or the 'Cherokee Advocate'.

"How come you're so interested in a bank?" Arnest asked Jean.

"Well," she answered, "it occurred to me that we are going to have a whole lot different situation in California than we did in Licklog. At Licklog, as soon as we gathered some gold or gold-quartz we could exchange it at the temporary mint that the U. S. Government set up in town. There was a bank in town where you could open an account and put your money there. That was civilization. Sutter's Mill is a long way away from civilization and when we find gold we're going to have to protect it 24 hours a day. It's going to be a different way of life," Jean predicted.

For the first time in this long trek, the Cherokee group actually looked at their water bags that Bixby had created for them at Fort Lupton. They only carried about two gallons of water on each side—four gallons total for a person and a horse. A working horse was supposed to be able to survive on one gallon of water a day, and a human being was supposed to be able to survive on one quart a day. Since each Cherokee had two horses (eight gallons of water), they should be able to survive for six to seven days on the water they carried. If they traveled 30 miles a day, the limitation of six or seven days was no problem—but what if their travel rate decreased to five or ten miles a day?

Bixby insisted that there would be portions of the trek where there was no local water available, but these treks were no more than 40 to 50 miles long. He insisted that one person with two horses and eight gallons of water could survive a 50 mile trek. These discussions were enough to cause one's throat to become very dry very quickly.

At Fort Bridger a local rancher told Jean and Howey that they would have to find some kind of a bag to hold grass for the animals because there would be times when the forage along the sides of the trail west of Salt Lake City played-out. If you had a wagon then that wagon would become your storage place for animal feed, but the Cherokees had no wagon. When the group got to Salt Lake City they explored the local stores to find something suitable. The local merchants were not very helpful. Then one lady in Salt Lake City's only cigar store (Tim and Bixby liked an occasional cigar at the end of a long day's ride and their supply was running low) remembered that there was a store on the west end of town that sold knitted bags for storing potatoes and onions. The bags were not very big, but they each had a drawstring at the top and could be ganged-together to store forage. Howey had brought a small scythe at Fort Lupton to cut grass, so now they could put the scythe to use.

No one had any idea of how many of these potato bags they should buy, so they bought two for each animal (12 horses and 4 mules, or 32 potato bags). They proved to be extremely valuable on the remainder of the trip west.

🍁   🍁   🍁

The salvation of the trek between Salt Lake City and the Sierra Nevada Mountains was supposed to be the Humboldt River, a river that flowed east to west, from an open sinkhole 200 miles west of Salt Lake City to another sinkhole 80 miles from the Truckee Pass. The Humboldt was 250 miles long. This was the only path to reach California by way of the 'central portal'. On the south side of the Hulmboldt there was barren desert, and on the north side of the Humboldt there were mountains that could not be traversed with wagons or animals.

Just getting to the start of the Humboldt River from Salt Lake City would have been a heroic task, had it not been for the Mormon Army. The Cherokee group found signs along the way pointing to water wells along the trail, in the desert, all dug by Mormon soldiers who were serving their military duty with the local militia. Sure enough, at each well site there was a sign that asked each group to 'dig the well deeper, for the next travelers', and the Cherokees tried to do their part. The wells were about 4 ft by 4 ft, and varied in depth from 10 to 30 feet. At one of the wells where they stopped there was no water in the well at all. By digging down two more feet, the group found no water, so they gave up on this well. At the next well they found an Army squad digging the well deeper, so they joined in the dig. This particular well already had about three or four inches of water in the bottom, and by the time the well was dug two feet deeper, it had almost six inches of water in the bottom. The water was full of minerals and had a slight sulfur taste to it, but it was potable.

Arnest told the soldiers about the dry well just 11 miles to the east, and the Sergeant in charge told him that his group was going to that well next. They were working their way east so they could finish up near Salt Lake City in about 10 or 12 days. The Cherokees asked the soldiers if this was as hot as it gets, and the answer was "No, the afternoons get hotter and hotter until middle September, then the temperature begins to slack-off."

Arnest could understand why there were soldiers working on the trail between Fort Bridger and Salt Lake City because that trail was full of Mormons coming from the East. But what Arnest could not understand was why Mormon soldiers would be digging water wells west of Salt Lake City (in some cases 200 miles west). There were no Mormon travelers here.

The Sergeant in charge of the troop had an answer for Arnest's question: "Lots of people have asked us about that. Brigham Young always says that we can't stop the emigrants from coming to Salt Lake City from the East, but we can help them in every way possible to keep them moving to the west when they reach the Great Salt Lake. The last thing we Mormons want is to have hundreds of thousands of emigrants who are non-Mormons deciding to settle in the Utah Territory. There isn't room for that many people out here. We need to keep everybody moving west!"

When they were100 miles west of Salt Lake City an incident occurred that made the Cherokees realize how fragile their existence in this desert really was. One evening, just as everyone was preparing to sleep, the horses caused a commotion and Arnest ran to the makeshift corral where the horses were located. He caught a young Indian trying to take the hobble off one of the young Morgan mares, and dragged him to the campfire by his hair to look at him more clearly. Everyone else in the party grabbed their firearms and prepared for the worst, but there apparently were no more Indians in the area.

There was no reason to talk to the young brave because he did not understand Cherokee or English. Bixby went over to his mules and brought a rope back to the campfire. He carefully began making a noose. Jean stepped between Bixby and the youth and told him in no uncertain terms that there would be no hanging of a youngster like this one tonight. So Bixby took his knife and quickly cut off the last quarter-inch of the boy's pinky finger. It immediately began to bleed and the kid broke loose from Arnest and ran. No one chased him, and in a couple of minutes all was peaceful.

But would it remain peaceful? Everyone spent the rest of the night wide awake, listening for the sound of an approaching Indian war party. But no war party came, and at the break of dawn the group was ready to move west.

There were very few trees along the Humboldt River, and those that existed were scrawny oak trees no more than ten feet tall. Early in the afternoon the group approached a lonely scrub oak, and there was a small body hanging from the top limb. Someone had tied the victim's hands behind him and hung him. When the Cherokees got close they realized that the victim was the same young brave that had attempted to steal one of their horses last night. Apparently he had tried one more theft last night, and that was his last.

"We will never know who the real villain in this story is," Jean commented. "Even out here in this god-forsaken wilderness there are Indians who can't survive unless they steal. They didn't pick this location as their favorite living spot—someone drove them out here and now they have become the despicable tribes of the great basin. This didn't have to happen."

❧   ❧   ❧

The Mormon soldiers told the Cherokees that they would know when they reached the mysterious bog that marked the start of the Humboldt River. The streams that fed the Humboldt at the east end were visible at times of the year, and then moved underground at other times of the year. Sometimes the water just seemed to emerge out of the ground, and began making its way west over a creekbed that must be hundreds of thousands of years old. They also told the Cherokees that the name of the Humboldt River was changed every few years by the map-makers, and then was changed to something else by the next map-maker. Mr. Humboldt was a German botanist (or something like that), and no one knew what he had to do with a waterway in the Nevada Territory. There certainly weren't any Germans living along the Humboldt River. No one lived along the Humboldt River.

The soldiers were right. On the eighteenth day out of Salt Lake City they reached a Mormon well that had a sign on it telling them that that this was the last of the desert wells. The Cherokees dug about four hours to deepen the well. Every time they left a well they filled up every water container they had, but this time they were especially careful to top-off all the water bags.

During the trek from Salt Lake City to the eastern edge of the Great Salt Desert they had passed four wagon trains. The Cherokees were moving faster than the wagon trains, but not as fast as they wanted. Oxen were famous for always traveling at a rate of two miles per hour, rain or shine, hot or cold. When it came time to pull the wagons up an incline, the usual six oxen per wagon were augmented to eight or ten. They made pretty good time going up the incline, but the oxen had to be returned to drag a second conestoga wagon up the same incline. So instead of making 20 miles a day (the rate that most wagonmasters wanted), they made 10 miles that day.

Since rivers don't change in 'height-above-sea-level' very fast, following a river was comforting to most travelers. It was when the rivers quit or headed up into the mountains that the settlers got worried. Waterfalls were the most terrifying obstacle—it might take a twenty mile detour and a week's lost time to go around a waterfall.

Thirty miles and two days past the last Mormon well, the Cherokees realized that there was a dark brown spot on the floor of the desert ahead. It was several miles across. Howey examined the dark brown spot carefully with his high-powered binoculars, and announced that they were at the famous starting point of the Humboldt River. This was where the river should appear. The soldiers had warned them to remain on the north side of the 'sink' and stay away from the dark brown sand because it became 'boggy' in a hurry. Conestoga wagons were especially vulnerable to the 'sink' with their narrow wheels and heavy weight.

As they were passing the bog they saw two small streams approaching the Humboldt from the north, and they were able to confirm their position on Bixby's rawhide map. Bixby was pleased with his guidework, and immediately after they crossed the second stream, they header southwest to join the main stream of the Humboldt. Once they reached the Humboldt they set the horses into the stream and walked the horses downstream, toward the west. It was great to find flowing water again, even though the water was murky and foul-smelling!

While they were at Fort Bridger, Tim and Bixby had spent a lot of time with an old trapper who claimed to have returned from the California Territory in the past year. He spoke disparagingly of the Humboldt River, claiming that the water was more 'rocky wet mud' than water, and the river wound around tight left-hand and right-hand curves endlessly. He claimed that sometimes they traveled 50 miles at the edge of the stream to get 20 miles farther west.

Everything the old trapper said was true. In the next twenty days the group must have traveled well over 400 miles along the river, but they probably only moved west by 200 miles. The streambed was full of rounded rocks set into the streambed. The horses liked the relative coolness of the water but the rocks were too slippery for the horses. After one of the horses crashed to the earth in the riverbed, the Cherokees decided to track along the edge of the river (rather than travel in the river). There were a few 'narrows' in the streambed where rock ledges along the edge prevented the group from traveling on the edge of the stream, but the narrows were few and far between.

Staufo and Renwe were angry about the fact that the Humboldt River kept meandering a little to the north, then a little to the south, then a little to the west, and on occasion, a little back to the east. The old man at Fort Bridger told them that the river was like a giant serpent, always making you think that the end of the bends in the river was just a few miles ahead. Then you kept confronting the bends, day after day after day. So the two young men devised a plan whereby they rode up and out of the stream and onto the plateau of sand and rock that was only twenty feet or so above the river. One horseman would remain there and the other one would move generally west to find where the river was when it 'snaked' back on itself. The plan worked pretty well. In some cases they only had to ride a hundred yards to the west over a sand plateau to find the next 'snake' of the river, whereas the path along the river was three to four hundred yards long. So this became the standard procedure for getting past the Humboldt River in a hurry. The secret to working this plan was to make sure that the next time the river 'snaked' back on itself, a horseman would be able to go down the sandy incline safely and return to the river. If you stayed up on the sandy plateau above the river and couldn't get down to the river, you were in trouble. This was the kind of maneuver they never could have made if they had a wagon—only horses and mules could do this 'skip-over-the-bends and plateaus' routine.

The small sand plateaus on either side of the river gave protection from the sun in the early morning and late in the day. But from mid-morning to mid-afternoon there was no way to hide from the sun. The only thing that kept everyone moving westward was the thought that this agony had to end sooner or later—other wagon trains had followed this trail to California and they had successfully made this part of the trip. The Cherokee group was buoyed by the fact that the wagon trains only covered half the distance every day that the Cherokees and their horses did.

Meanwhile, the water in the river became more and more acrid, and Arnest began to wonder how long the horses would swallow the 'stratified mud' they were offered. Horses know how to complain, and complain they did! They would sample the water, snort loudly, look to their left and their right for something better to drink, and then take a few swallows from the river. Bixby's mules seemed to accept the acrid water better than the horses—maybe they were used to being treated badly. Bixby always insisted that mules tolerated bad travel a lot better than horses did. They were 'not so persnickety'.

No one in the Cherokee band violated the water rules during this time of acrimony. Everyone lived with one quart of water a day, and their animals were given small amounts of water from the water bags. There was no guarantee that the Humboldt would continue to provide water to the group, so most of the water in the bags had to be kept for emergencies.

They passed five wagon trains while they were following the Humboldt River. At night they would camp close to a wagon train for security reasons. The wagon train settlers always assumed that if they were attacked it would be by some local Indians—not by another wagon train group. By the time the Cherokees cleared the first hundred miles of the Humboldt they realized that there probably were no more Indians along the trail—surviving in this area was just too tough for man or beast.

The only local source of water for the animals was the river, and the Cherokees tried to pick a campsite every evening where there was some forage for the animals. 'Forage' in this case didn't mean real grass—it meant a kind of 'saw grass' that was growing between rocks. It was extremely tough to cut, and equally as tough for the animals to chew. But 'chew' they did! As a last resort, if no forage was found, the Cherokees would give each animal two large handfuls of the grass they had cut in Salt Lake City. That was all the grass they could spare for one evening.

One evening, when Jean walked over to a nearby wagon train camped on a sandbar to ask how things were going for them, one of the men in the wagon train ran quickly to his wagon, removed his rifle, and glared at Renwe and Staufo (who were walking with their mother). The Cherokees had dark skins, but the glare of the sun in this desert country gave every wagon train emigrant a dark skin. Some of the whites were badly sunburned (including Tim Wisnant, who resorted to applying the Venice Turpentine horse-hoof ointment that he bought from St. Louis to his face and hands every day. But he still looked like an over-ripe turnip).

When the man with his rifle raised the issue with Jean about the 'Indians' who were with her, she simply told them that they were her sons, and yes, they were Indians—Cherokee Indians. Then she asked the man why he kept his rifle 'at the ready' while the Cherokees stood in front of their fire and talked peace. The wagon train hadn't seen a Plains Indian for over 200 miles, and probably wouldn't see any Indians until they crossed the Sierra Nevada Mountains.

Was the man really afraid that an Indian war party was going to emerge over the top of the next sand dune? She ended the conversation with "No self-respecting Indian would come within a hundred miles of this god-forsaken place, and we all know that." The group of settlers around her all agreed with her statement and life returned back to normal.

Between Fort Bridger and Salt Lake City there were occasional 'crosses' pounded into the earth beside the trail to show the burial place of an emigrant. No one had the equipment to write the person's name on the cross—they were unmarked. There were also occasional dumpings of furniture that could no longer be carried in some emigrant's wagon—the oxen or mules were beginning to 'crack' under the load of the wagons and the family's finest furniture had to be left behind. The wagonmaster had probably told these emigrants to leave all the furniture behind in St. Joseph, Missouri, but no one would listen.

There were stories in Salt Lake City about a group of furniture salesmen who traveled the Mormon, California, and Oregon trails to pick up this abandoned furniture, and returned it to Salt Lake City for re-sale. Consequently, some of the wealthier homes in Salt Lake City were outfitted with the finest East Coast furniture available.

The 'crosses' began to appear again while the Cherokees were following the Humboldt River, and after following the Humboldt for 100 miles the crosses appeared at every major bend in the river. When the crosses disappeared it meant only one thing: the emigrants had run out of wood to mark the graves. The dead (mostly children) were now lowered into shallow graves and marked only with a piece of a scrub oak tree.

Seeing the never-ending crosses was almost more than Jean could bear. The graves were short—showing that the body buried beneath the sand was a little person—a child. "Can you imagine," she said to Arnest and Howey, "how it would be to give birth to a child, raise that child up to the point where they walked and talked and skipped on their own, and then you brought them on a long trip across the American deserts and watched them die. They died slowly from lack of food and warm clothing, or they died fast from the bite of an adder or a snake."

She continued with: "At every one of these grave markers, some woman and some man stood there and asked themselves, 'Why did we ever bring this child to this place to die? Why were we so stupid?'

Bixby had told everyone in the Cherokee group how they would know that they were at the end of the Humboldt River—the river would disappear into a sinkhole just like the one at the eastern end of the river. This sinkhole would be bigger than the one at the start of the river. Sure enough, on the 21st of September the Humboldt River disappeared into the boggy desert. This was the famous Humboldt Sinkhole. No one knew where the water from the river went to. Off to the west, the peaks of the Sierra Nevada loomed. It was well over a hundred degrees along the sinkhole, but there was snow on the peaks of all the mountains to the west.

That evening, just before sundown, Bixby took an ancient compass out of his saddlebags and began looking at the mountains to the west. The sun was about to go behind the mountains, so all that could be seen on the horizon was a series of dark grey peaks with snow spots along the top. Bixby told the group that tomorrow he would set a course for 220 degrees from the south edge of the Humboldt Sinkhole, and they would follow that course for 35 miles to find the Truckee River. Once they found the Truckee they would follow it all the way to the top of the pass through the Sierra Nevadas and into California.

It sounded like a pretty easy job, but Bixby warned them that the desert they were going to cross had no landmarks whatsoever—the group had to keep their eyes on one of the peaks of the Sierra Nevada and head for it. That was easily done in the daylight, but their chances of keeping the animals alive were much better at night. So Bixby made the decision that they were going to travel at night. The total length of the trek was only 35 miles, which they could cover from sundown one day to noon the next day—but they had to keep moving at all times and hold a 220 degree course to the southwest. If high winds came up they would have to blindfold the animals and guide them while walking—you can't ride a horse or mule in the middle of a sandstorm.

When the sun came up the next morning the group was exposed to the most intensive heat they had seen so far. There wasn't anything anyone could do to make the situation better, so they just kept walking. No one rode their animals much of that day, and both humans and animals kept their eyes as tightly shut as possible to keep out the swirling sand.

During a pause in the trek, while the group stood under a group of forlorn palm trees to get out of the sun, Renwe spotted a large snake that objected to their passing by. When the Cherokees got closer to the snake it started moving sideways by a series of quick coil and then un-coil movements. Later on they found that this was the famous 'sidewinder' rattle snake. It was scary when the animal remained in a fixed position, but it was really scary when the animal decided to move.

By evening of the second day Bixby spotted the Truckee River. He wanted to get the group into the protective walls of the Truckee Canyon quickly so they would not be harassed with high winds and blowing sand. The Truckee River had good water in it, so everyone had to stop and wash off some of the sand and the grime from their long trip from Salt Lake City. Bixby didn't allow them to remain there for long because he knew there were better camping places just 40 miles up the river, in a place called the 'Truckee Meadows'.

A day and a half later they reached the Truckee Meadows, and they rested for two days there. Bixby explained that 'Truckee' was a Paiute Indian who began leading wagon trains from this spot where they were camping to a release point about 40 miles west (in the California Territory). The Donner Party had camped here on October 24, and spent seven days here before beginning the 1200 foot climb to the start of the pass. The pass is only 7,000 ft high, and the land they were camping on was at about 5,000 ft, so moving through Truckee Pass was no great challenge—right?

Apparently the worst snow storm in the history of the Sierra Nevadas caught the Donner Group just 15 miles into the pass, at the high point in the pass. They were only 20 miles away from safety when the storm hit, but could not proceed. The storm blocked their retreat to the east and their escape to the west.

No one in the Cherokee group wanted to spend any time in the Truckee Pass, knowing what a snowstorm had done to the Donner Group three years earlier—less than half of the party survived the snowstorm. However, the Cherokees were at the pass nearly a month earlier in the season than the Donner Group.

That evening, as the sun was setting behind the Sierra Nevada Mountains, Arnest and Jean sat down with their boys to find out if they were doing alright at this stage of the trip. Arnest began the conversation with, "Renwe, are you sorry that you decided to come on this trip?"

Renwe thought for a moment, and then returned with "No, Father, I don't think so. I hope this is as bad as it gets, though. Bixby says that the worst is over, and I'm glad. I hate to think about making this trip again when we decide to go back home some day, though."

Staufo was thinking about other things: "In the last 200 miles we have passed nine wagon trains that are on their way to the gold fields. Lookin' up there at the Truckee Pass, I know we'll do alright because we are fast and we're a small group. We don't have any cattle or sheep to push through that pass either. I wonder if one of those nine wagon trains will be caught in the pass just like the Donner Group, and perish in the mountains."

"Do the white crosses next to the trail bother you?" Jean asked.

"I'm glad I didn't know any of those people who died," Staufo said. "I am especially glad that we don't have any children with us, because they would probably be the first to die."

"Renwe," Arnest asked, "did the young brave who tried to steal one of our horses get 'justice' back there on the Humboldt River?"

Renwe was slow to answer. "I guess if you spend your lifetime stealing horses then sooner or later you're going to get hung by some angry horse owner. I kept asking myself, when we saw the body hanging from the tree, 'why did that brave steal a horse?' Was this the only way he could get an animal to ride, out here in this snake-infested desert? Then I asked myself, 'If his family was in this terrible situation out here on the desert, why didn't they just keep traveling west into California, and settle down somewhere else?'"

Arnest and Jean nodded in agreement.

Staufo answered Renwe's question in part when he suggested, "Maybe the Indians went west, and somebody in California ran them off and forced them back onto the desert. Maybe the Indians and the Mexicans on the other side of the Sierra Nevada Mountains are bigger, stronger, and meaner than the Indians here on the desert.

Jean spoke: "The Cherokees have never been bigger, stronger, or meaner than other groups of people around them, yet we have survived where other tribes have failed. We have had to live 'smarter', Renwe, and don't you ever forget it. You must live by your wits, not by your physical strength. And that doesn't mean that you 'cheat' the people around you who are less smart than you are—you have to deal fairly with everyone."

❦   ❦   ❦

At daybreak, just as the party was preparing to begin the ascent to the Truckee Pass, a small group of Indians approached the campsite. They looked peaceful enough, and there were only five of them. One was a young brave who was riding a small paint pony. Tim had spent a good part of the past evening examining the hooves of the animals, and one of the older mares was in trouble. Her hooves were breaking-down badly, and she needed to spend several months to recuperate. Tim and Arnest agreed that the animal should not be ridden by anyone and it should carry a minimum of camping gear. They just hoped that the animal would survive for the last leg of this journey to the Sutter Mill.

When the Indians approached, Arnest was not sure what to do. The Chief in the group made several signs with his hands and the Cherokees tried to figure out what he was asking. Bixby came to the rescue: "He wants to guide us through the pass," Bixby stated. What to do?

Tim had the answer; he moved up quickly between Arnest and Jean and began to speak with both of them. Arnest and Jean were agreeing with him, whatever he was saying. Tim reached in the saddlebags of his second horse and extracted a can of salve used to treat the animals' hooves. Then he took Renwe's second horse (the mare with the major hoof problems) and led the mare over to the young brave. He removed the saddlebags, the potato bags, and the water bags from behind the mare's saddle and placed them on his pack horse. Then he motioned for the young brave to come to the Morgan, and once he was there, Tim raised the animal's right front hoof. He showed the young man the gashes in the hoof, opened the can of salve, and placed some of it in the cuts. Then he went to the other three hoofs and repeated the process. When he was finished he closed the can of salve, gave it to the young man, and handed him the reins to the mare. Then Tim returned to his paint horse and mounted the animal.

The Indian Chief was pleased. He handed Howey a smoked shoulder from a small animal (like a deer)—the Cherokees hadn't eaten real meat in over three weeks! Then he pointed to two young braves who immediately positioned themselves to lead the group into the pass. With a wave, the other Indians turned and left the Meadows. The last horse in their group was the old Morgan mare, making its way carefully along the path. Arnest always shed a tear when he had to part with one of his beloved Morgans, but this time it had to be.

It was September 30, 1849, and the Cherokees were about to enter the Promised Land.

CHAPTER 8

California Here We Come

Once the group cleared the Truckee Pass they were only 80 miles from Sutter's Mill. The Paiute guides remained with them for two days, and then indicated that it was time for them to return to their village on the other side of the Sierra Nevada. As a parting gift, the brave who was leading the group took them slightly off the trail to a small meadow where excellent grass was growing. While the animals were foraging, the brave disappeared into a tiny box canyon and emerged with a handful of apples. Apparently he was the only one who knew about this secret supply of fresh apples, and he chose to share some of them with the Cherokees. As soon as he had passed out the apples he and his partner waved goodbye and headed back home. Their job was done.

Two days later the Cherokees arrived at the Mexican village of Coloma, where the mill was located. Sutter's chief builder, Mr. Marshall, had decided to build the sawmill on a big ninety-degree turn in the American River, as it turned from a northwesterly direction to a southwesterly direction. Two hundred yards later it resumed the march to the northwest. It took a lot of water, moving as fast as possible, to rotate the undershot wheel mounted below the main cutting deck of the sawmill. Marshall's men (a group of Mormon men who had finished fighting the Mexican War and were headed for Salt Lake City when they got an offer from Sutter to build the sawmill) dammed the entire river (about 100 feet wide) so all the water would pass through the spillway. When the spillway and sawmill were close to completion, Mr. Marshall observed tiny, shiny nuggets of ore that passed through the almost-completed tailrace, and he picked up a few to show to Sutter. A hundred yards downstream of the mill he found other small nuggets and was convinced that the ore was gold. The Mormons were convinced also. They finished the mill because they had contracted to do so, but they also panned for gold every free moment they had. As soon as the mill was completed they panned for gold twenty-four hours a day.

Sutter tried to keep the gold find a secret, but the word got out.

The American River was shallow—no more than two feet deep at most places. So the first gold hunters used simple metal pans to 'pan' for gold. Other more sophisticated methods of panning for gold were invented almost on a weekly basis, and soon the river was filled with 'cradles' (rocked from side to side to remove the soft sediment in the sample being checked for gold), 'long-toms' and 'sluices' (inclined troughs with nails in the bottom that stopped the heavy metals from sliding down the trough while the sand and other lighter particles were washed down the trough and finally dumped at the end by the river current). Miners dumped buckets full of the fine gravel in the streambed into the top of the trough and agitated the gravel so the moving current of the river would wash away the sand. From time to time they examined the remains at the bottom of the trough for gold nuggets or very small particles classified as 'gold dust'.

About 200 yards downstream from the sawmill spillway, the American River separated into two streams and moved around a small island in the middle. The island was 'Mormon Island', so named because this was where the Mormon Battalion set up housekeeping to build the sawmill and later pan for gold. The sawmill was used to cut lumber for less than a month, even though lumber was in great demand throughout the gold field. No one would work for Sutter while there was gold to be had.

The most unusual aspect of the sawmill was that the cutting blade was a vertically-mounted, reciprocal blade nearly seven feet long, not a rotary blade such as was found in the mountains of the Southeastern part of the country. The blade would cut into the log on its downward stroke.

Even though Sutter had a working agreement with the Mexican Government before the Mexican War of 1847, he had never been able to get a deed to the land near Coloma where the sawmill was built. When the Mexican Govern-ment ceded the territory to the USA in 1848, Sutter was no more successful in getting a deed for his sawmill land than from the Americans than we was with the Mexicans. So he was caught in the terrible situation where fortunes were being made all around the sawmill and he had no part in it. The land was always considered to be U. S. property.

The local Mexicans and Indians came to pan for gold as families, and they were much more careful to snatch every tiny piece of gold out of the river as they 'panned' and 'sluiced'. Not so with the groups who were arriving daily from San Francisco, Monterrey, all the tiny villages up and down the California Ter-ritory, and the wagon trains arriving from the East. These people were inter-ested in the big nuggets of gold (which were plentiful at first) and they disdained the small particles of gold dust.

By asking around, the Cherokees found that you could buy the equipment used to pan for gold either in Coloma (the site of Sutter's sawmill), or in a town ten miles south named Hangtown. But there was no use to buy gold min-ing equipment if the Cherokee group couldn't get a 'claim' or 'placer' that pro-duced gold.

The areas upstream and downstream of the mill, for a distance of about a mile, were filled with dingy white tents on the sides of the river and men with large felt hats out in the river, plying their gold mining trade. All the Cherokee group could do for now was to set up a base camp far from the river and find the U. S. Government office that issued legal claims to the 'placers'.

Then they found out that there was no 'U. S. Government office' that issued gold claims, and the edges of each claim were not surveyed-in (as they had been at Licklog). The corners of one's claim were marked with poles made from small trees, hammered into the riverbed. The claims (also called 'placers') near the Sutter Mill were no more than 25 feet by 25 feet. The sheriff of the town of Coloma, Sheriff Rogers, had become alarmed at the high incidence of 'claim jumping', so he initiated a process where each person's claim was regis-tered at the Sheriff's Office (Coloma was the county seat—the county had changed its name to 'Eldorado County', in honor of the mythical Mexican 'city of gold' that the Spanish explorers had sought for several centuries). The Rogers family owned the Rogers Hotel on Main Street.

While the Cherokees were walking over the area downstream of the sawmill they passed by an older Chinese man who was engaged in an argument with two white men. Arnest stopped to listen to the argument, and soon realized that the argument was about the Chinaman's claim to the placer where he was standing. When the white men realized that Arnest and Howey were listening to the conversation they turned and left the premises.

Arnest and Howey asked the Chinese man what you had to do to stake a claim in this gold rush, and the man directed them to a large shed about a quarter of a mile downstream from where they were standing. The shed was on a small bluff about 100 yards back from the river. The man suggested that he and Arnest should talk about the situation here in Coloma before Arnest filed a claim with the county, because there was a lot happening at the gold site. There probably were a lot of 'placers' left on the county's list, but only a few of them would ever produce gold.

The Chinese man introduced himself as Chin Zhou. He and his family worked four placers. He had three sons and a daughter. They had been on site, about 100 yards downstream of Mormon Island, for about 15 months now. The main thing he wanted to tell Arnest was that the claim next to his might be for sale or lease because the family who owned it had been beset with two deaths in the family and they were anxious to return to San Francisco. They were the O'Leary family and had also been on site for about 15 months. The easiest way to get into the gold-panning business was to make a deal with the neighbor (Mr. O'Leary) such that the Simmons family would take over the gold-panning business and split the gold 50—50 with the O'Leary family. This was the common way for a gold claim to change hands in the American River valley.

He also told Arnest that the Simmons family should file claims of their own with the county, if for no other reason than to have a piece of land to build a cabin on. His family lived in tents, but Chin told Arnest that this was the wrong thing to do. "Build a permanent cabin, and build it soon," he told Arnest. "The rainy season comes soon. The land next to the river is handy for gold-panning, but the river runs over its banks every spring and destroys most of the long-toms and sluices in the river channel. In late fall and the winter everyone has to move back from the river's edge—else they live in a sea of mud."

Chin pointed to several dingy white tents that were pitched right along the edge of the river, and told Arnest that these tents would have to be moved from the present river edge or they would be washed downstream as soon as the rains came.

Then Chin invited the Cherokees to stay for supper that night, and he suggested that they place their animals in a temporary corral that the Zhou family had built on the bank of the river. When he saw the Morgan horses he said that these horses would catch the eye of the horse thieves who were all over the area, and they should be guarded carefully.

That evening the Cherokee group was introduced to the Zhou family: The father, Chin, the three sons, Ho, Kim, and Yang, and a daughter, We Sa. The boys were in their early twenties and We Sa was a teenager. Chin explained that his wife was unable to come to the gold fields.

Late that evening the Cherokee group met behind the Zhou corral, and decided to follow Mr. Zhou's advice. For one thing, the group had spent more money than they planned, and they probably were not in a position to buy anyone's claim outright. For a second thing, the claim that they might be assigned to them by the county now (where there were hundreds of people everywhere, all searching for gold) might be miles and miles away from the sawmill and the river. Chin had said that the O'Leary placer was bringing in gold daily, and splitting the take 50—50 might make more money for the Simmons than mining in a totally new placer.

CHAPTER 9

Setting-Up Housekeeping

The next day Arnest, Howey, Renwe, Staufo, Bixby, and Tim did exactly what Chin suggested. They went to the county land-claims office just south of Mormon Island and applied for a placer for each. There were maps posted on the walls everywhere inside the building, and they included the American River, every tributary that flowed into the American River, and every river that flowed into the Sacramento River (both north and south of Old Sacramento City).

The county agent also told the men that there were placers available far south, near the 'Mariposa' region, but they would have to go there to file claims. All the claims were on federal land. The Cherokees found out later that the 'Mariposa' was land that was given to the Fremont family after John Fremont conducted surveying expeditions in the far west, and the problem in the Mariposa was that many newcomers were 'jumping' from federal land to Fremont's claim and mining gold there illegally.

The six men found that there were placers unclaimed within 200 yards of the Zhou campsite, but they were situated far away from the river in every case. So the group decided to wait until the next day to file claims—tomorrow they would try to reach an agreement with the O'Leary family to take over their claim and split the gold.

The next day, when Arnest was ready to speak to Mr. O'Leary, Chin suggested that he accompany Arnest to the main tent of the O'Leary family and make introductions. He and O'Leary had become good friends over the past 15 months, and plenty of people had offered to buy the claim or split the gold with old man O'Leary, but he didn't trust any of them. It remained to be seen if O'Leary trusted the Cherokees.

"Why would these people want to lease their claim?" Arnest asked. "If it's making money for them, why would they want to leave the settlement?" Chin explained that the O'Leary family had experienced two deaths in the past three months—both of them at their home in San Francisco. "They want to get back home before anything else bad happens."

"Do bad things happen around here?" Arnest asked.

Chin was slow to answer: "There's a lot more occurrences of shootings and fights in this settlement than there used to be, but that's because people are pouring in from everywhere and they all come for the same reason—gold. The Sheriff told us the other day that there were 40,000 people in the county searching for gold, and most of them are going to be sorely disappointed."

When they approached the main tent on the O'Leary claim a woman came out and greeted Chin and Arnest. Chin introduced Arnest to the woman as the leader of a group of Cherokees that had come from the Cherokee Nation Territory to mine for gold. Her name was Irene.

"You picked a good time to come to the Mill," Irene told Arnest. "You can build a place to live-in before the rains come. We decided to live in tents, and that was a big mistake."

Then she added: "The way you see these tents sprinkled all over the water's edge and into the trees set back from the river, you gotta figure that the owners of the placers consider this a very temporary place to live. It will be funny if some of these 'yayhoos' are still here five years from now."

Arnest explained that they were hoping that his group could work the O'Leary claim and split the gold with the O'Leary family. They didn't have enough money to buy a claim outright, and most of the claims that the county was issuing were at places far away from the Sutter Mill.

"I'll be back in a minute," she told the men. Then she walked over to the edge of the river, lifted her skirts, and walked over to a long-tom where two people were working. She spoke with a large man with a scraggly white beard, and shortly the two of them walked back to the tent.

"Mr. Simmons," Irene said, "this here is my husband, John O'Leary. John, Arnest Simmons."

The two men shook hands. "Irene tells me that you want to make a deal with us to mine the gold in our claim. It's probably a good idea. We're getting a lot more gold out of this river than most people."

Then he added, "Let's go inside the tent and talk."

With Chin's continual prodding, a deal was struck after a full afternoon of negotiations. The O'Learys would keep the placers in their name and return to San Francisco in the next two weeks. They would leave all their mining equipment behind, but none of their animals. They would take all their cooking and sleeping gear and firearms back to San Francisco. They would leave any foodstuffs behind, but O'Leary warned Arnest that this may only amount to a few bags of rice and potatoes, a little smoked bacon, and a generous supply of soy sauce for cooking. "We cook everything around here in soy sauce," he mentioned.

The oldest son in the O'Leary family, Hubert, would appear at the placer on the first day of each month and Arnest would present him with half of the gold they had mined the past month. Mr. O'Leary knew what that amount should be because their gold production from the placers had been fairly constant for the past six months.

The O'Learys wanted to return to San Francisco in two weeks, so they offered to teach the Cherokees everything they knew about panning and sluicing for gold. John O'Leary pointed out the location of his placers, in the middle of the river. The four claims were arranged in a nose-to-tail fashion, so their total claim was 25 feet wide by 100 feet long. The fence posts that marked the corners of the claim had been pounded into the riverbed.

So, having settled this, the Cherokee men marched over to the Eldorado County Land-Claims Office to get new placers for themselves. The agent charged them a small fee to set the corners of the claim into the ground with aspen tree fence posts. Jean came with them this time so they could pore over the government maps some more, and by noon they had made their decisions. They signed up for four placers in a square (2 by 2) pattern, about 150 yards from the river centerline. There was a rock abutment square in the middle of the placers—it was the rock abutment that kept a thousand gold seekers before them from signing up for the placers. It was a poor place to mine for gold. The rock abutment was about 50 feet across (perpendicular to the stream) and 120 feet wide (parallel to the stream).

Since the four placers were not in the American River riverbed, they were larger in size. They were 50 feet wide and 50 feet long. There was plenty of room to construct a corral for the animals and a cabin to live in. The abutment stood about eight feet above the present water level of the American River, and Chin was sure that the spring rains would never undermine the cabin they planned to build. "You may have a little trouble sinking fence posts for the corral," Chin suggested, "but maybe not."

The county also gave them the deeds to two other placers nearly eight miles downstream of Mormon Island. They were also 50 feet by 50 feet. None of the placers in that area had produced any gold yet.

The distance from the four new Simmons placers to the center of the O'Leary placers was no more than 200 yards, so all the equipment used to keep the troughs working could be transported to the river every morning and returned to the cabin at night. If a piece of equipment was left on the edge of the river one evening, it was gone the next morning. If there was honor among the gold miners in the settlement it was not easily discernable.

The county agent had warned the Cherokees that it was important to work their claims on a daily basis, since a claim left unattended for more than two weeks was considered to be an 'abandoned claim'. If a new arrival could prove that a claim had been left unattended then the county would transfer the claim to the new arrival.

Arnest asked O'Leary if the land beneath his tents was part of his claim, and O'Leary said "No, they aren't. The fifty feet or so on both banks of the river is a flood plane, and the county won't issue any claims for those sites since they are common ground for tents, etc."

The rules were a little confusing, but they seemed to have some logic to them.

Jean had listened carefully when Chin spoke about the coming rainy season, and she was anxious to build a cabin for the group before those rains came. Since both Chin and O'Leary agreed that the Morgan horses were far too valuable to be neglected while everyone was building a cabin and a corral, Mr. O'Leary decided to make the Simmons family a present to confirm their agreement—he arranged for a 'stoker' to come in and brand all the Simmons, Wisnant, and Bixby animals. He also suggested that Chin have his animals branded because the incidence of horse thievery was increasing every month.

Bixby said 'thank you but no thank you' to the idea of branding his mules. He claimed that a mule was too tender-hearted to be inflicted with the searing pain of applying a brand to his rump. Howey and Chin came up with the idea of using a common 'brand' for both the Cherokee and the Zhou animals, and the brand turned out to be a small capital 'S', a space of about half an inch, and a small capital 'Z'.

The corral was built first because the presence of both the 'S' animals and the 'Z' animals at the Zhou corral was too much—the animals were constantly bumping into one-another. The side of the two Simmons placers that were the farthest from the river had some trees on them—which made them totally unacceptable as gold panning sites. But the lumber was great for making a corral—if only they could get the trees to a sawmill before the rains came. They also needed lumber for the cabin.

There were only two kinds of trees on the lot—cottonwoods and aspens. Neither tree was the kind that a cabin builder would pick for his home, but they had to do. The young aspen trees made good fence posts however. Renwe was especially fast at felling and clearing trees in preparation for saw milling into slab lumber, and he saw a chance to make some money at a nearby sawmill because he was so fast with an axe. The owner offered to pay him $7.00 a day (a ten-hour day) because no one would work for him long enough to learn the sawmill trade. The best money that Renwe ever made at home was a dollar a day to clear farm land.

So Renwe agreed to work for the sawmill owner if he would give him a special price for sawing the cottonwoods into slabs. The owner of the sawmill laughed at the idea, saying that cottonwoods made 'sorry' lumber and would never produce a durable cabin. So he offered a compromise—he would loan Renwe his big wagon to bring the cottonwood trees to his mill, and for every two cottonwoods that Renwe brought, the owner would slab one of his ponderosa pine trees. According to the locals, the ponderosa lumber was much better than the cottonwood lumber.

Renwe agreed to the deal after he spoke at length with his younger brother, Staufo, about felling the cottonwoods. Arnest, Howey, and Tim also agreed to fell some of the trees, but Bixby claimed that he had a nagging back injury several years ago that kept him from swinging an axe. After five days of intensive cutting, the proper number of cottonwoods were cut and trimmed for delivery to the sawmill. Then the aspens were cut and sized for fence posts.

Getting the cottonwood trees loaded onto the huge wagon was another problem, so the sawmill owner had to come to the Simmons claim and show the Cherokees how to build a 'ramp' to pull the logs up and into the wagon. After a log was lined up next to the ramp, two cables from the wagon were looped around the log and returned to the back side of the wagon where two giant Wisconsin draft horses were waiting to pull the log up the ramp. They rolled the log into the wagon without even breaking a sweat.

The owner of the sawmill was a man of his word—two days after the cottonwoods were delivered to the sawmill site he delivered the slabbed pine trees to the cabin site. He even threw-in a lightweight front door with iron hinges. Arnest bought enough cut nails to put the cabin together and Howey borrowed two hammers from a nearby family (by offering them a half-dozen cigars made in Havana. He had carried these cigars all the way from Salt Lake City).

Since Renwe and Staufo were so busy preparing the lumber for the cabin and corral, it fell to Arnest and Howey to hunt for small game in the local area for food. Neither one of them was a good shot, so they came back empty-handed most of the time. Meanwhile, Jean met a young man who sold Rhode Island Red chickens for a dollar apiece (going from door to door), and she provided the fresh meat for the evening meal.

Everyone in the Cherokee group seemed to be content with the idea that they were not panning for gold—yet. The O'Leary family had not cleared the premises, and the biggest worry at the time for the Cherokees was that the lumber to build the cabin would not arrive on site before the rains came.

It took three days to build the corral and three weeks to build the cabin. The only pressing (and unanswered) question that the Cherokee group had when it came to cabin building in California was this: What to use for a roof on the cabin? A cabin wasn't much use unless it has a good roof. In the East the standard roof was cedar shingle, but there didn't seem to be any cedar shingles for hundreds of miles around (this was not true—there were thousands of cedar shingles in southern California, several hundred miles away).

Fortunately tarpaper had already been invented several years earlier, and the general store in Coloma had plenty on hand. So the roof of the cabin was sheathed with the ratty pine lumber left over from the sawmill deal and tarpaper was placed over that. But how to nail the tarpaper down well enough that the wind wouldn't blow it away? The general store had cut nails to put pieces of lumber together, but no special nails with a big 'head' to keep tar-paper affixed to the roof sheathing. The only thing Arnest and Howey could do was to drive a cut nail half-way into the sheathing, then bend the nail over and hammer it into the tarpaper. Jean noticed that some of the Indians in the area had sod roofs, and she figured that the sod may not be waterproof but the tarpaper underneath was. Maybe the sod on top of the roof would keep the tarpaper from blowing away. They carefully cut blocks of sod about a foot square and two inches thick and transported them to the cabin site where they were placed on the tarpaper.

And none too soon! Only a week after the roof was placed on the cabin, the first big rain passed through the settlement. The rain was driven by high winds from the west, and drenched the settlement area completely. But the tarpaper held and the leaks in the cabin roof were minimal. There were some places in the cabin where you could sit during a rain and there were some places where you could *not* sit during a rain.

❧   ❧   ❧

Meanwhile, Jean had been thinking about the young man who brought a Rhode Island Red chicken to their cabin door and sold it to her for one dollar. The young man had never come back, and Jean missed the fresh chicken. So she asked around and found that the family of the young man lived almost fifteen miles away, clear on the other side of Hang Town. One day she and We Sa (Chin's daughter, the Zhou family cook), made the long trip to the young man's farm to find out how to buy more chickens. She was pleased to find out that there were many more Rhode Island Reds where the first one came from. She also spotted a dozen chicken cages on the farm, like the ones they had back home to transport chickens from place to place.

The family was the Parkers, originally from Illinois (twenty years ago). They had bought their farm from the Mexicans in 1829, and they wanted no part of the gold hunt. But they were willing to sell chickens to anyone who came to the farm, for one dollar apiece. If you wanted the chicken killed and plucked that was free, but most buyers wanted to keep the chicken alive as long as possible. The killing and plucking was done after the buyer arrived at his cabin, which could be a half-a-day's ride on a horse or mule.

This time she bought two live chickens, and asked the family how much they wanted for the old chicken coops. The Parkers had no use for the coops, so the agreed to sell them to her for two dollars apiece. Then they agreed to sell her 50 chickens at a time (ten chickens in each of five coops) for only $40.00. A money-making scheme was beginning to form in Jean's head, but she realized that she was lacking one item in the plan—a wagon strong enough to transport ten chicken coops from the Parker farm to her cabin at the settlement. The Parker family had no wagon that would do the job, and they had no idea of where to get one.

There were old conestoga wagons everywhere, but they were extremely heavy and took four oxen to pull. What Jean needed was a wagon half as heavy as a conestoga—one that could be pulled by two Morgan horses.

The O'Learys had vacated their tents at the American River and were ready to return to San Francisco. Arnest and Howey knew that they had to get serious about gold-panning because the oldest O'Leary son, Hubert, would return in 30 days to get half of the month's 'take' in gold. They had to have something to show for the month's work.

Tim had participated actively in the building of the cabin and the corral—he was proficient with a hammer. He also had a lot of cabin layout skills because he had built several 'slab cabins' near Fort Lupton in his life. He even knew about putting 'rice paper' in the window holes of the cabin so some light would come through and lighten-up the dark interior of the cabin.

Bixby, on the other hand, smashed his thumbs a few times with the hammer and sought a way to stay clear of the construction work. To his credit, he always made sure that all the animals were properly watered and taken into the woods to find suitable forage. The animals were beginning to show signs of recovering from the 2000 mile trip they had made from the Cherokee Nation Territory to central California.

When the rains came, Arnest learned the meaning of the words 'keep your powder dry' when he found water dripping onto the saddlebags that contained all their shot and black powder. The last thing he wanted to buy was more ammunition or powder, so he told everyone that he was going to dry-out the powder somehow and make it do until next spring. His plan didn't work.

Soon a sequence of daily tasks-to-be-performed evolved, and everyone found a way to stay busy. For example, Arnest, Howey, and Tim spent all their time on the troughs that the O'Learys had built in the river, and Jean spent all her time preparing food and washing clothes. Renwe had his job at the sawmill, which was great because this produced an immediate income to buy food, etc. Staufo, not to be undone, offered to tend the troughs in the river also, but Bixby beat him to the punch by working alongside Howey most of the time. Four men was enough to do the trough job, and Staufo knew it.

Staufo became a little angry because Renwe always had money to spend, and he (Staufo) had none. So the family wasn't all that surprised when Staufo reported that he got a job at a local wagon-works about six miles down the

American River. Jean's ears perked up because she was secretly searching for a lightweight wagon that could transport Rhode Island Red chickens between the Parker farm and the Simmons cabin. Staufo did not divulge the pay he was getting from the wagon-works, so the family figured that it was less than Renwe's $7.00 a day. Then they found out later that he was making more than Renwe, but he could keep more of his pay for himself by not admitting what his wage was.

The rains continued, the American River swelled past its banks, and it was clear that all the troughs would be lost if they weren't removed from the streambed quickly. So late one evening everyone pitched in and pulled the troughs out of the muck on the bottom of the river. It took longer than they expected, so they finished the job with one person holding a kerosene lantern high above their head while everyone else grunted and groaned to lift the troughs free from the river. Once this was done they took the troughs carefully back to a place behind the cabin. In five months they would need the troughs again.

When Hubert O'Leary showed up to get the first month's gold split he was satisfied with the 'take'. He knew that the start of the rainy season severely hampered the gold-hunting process every year, and he had come from San Francisco mostly to see if the Cherokees had any questions about running the claim. He explained that he was hoping for a windfall in gold profits in 1850 because he needed money to go to college soon. Apparently all the money the Cherokees were giving the O'Leary family were earmarked for higher education—mostly his.

The Zhou family moved into their 'winter home' a hundred feet or so back from the river's edge, just outside of the flood plane, and attempted to 'sluice' for gold even after the rains came. But the work proved to be quite dangerous and their youngest son, Yang, suffered a deep cut in his leg when the river bowled him over and thrust him upon some nearby rocks. For a while the cut would not heal, and the family watched him in dread that the tell-tale sign of blood poisoning would show around the edges of the wound. There was some reddening of the wound, but after two months the redness disappeared and the family knew that he would recover. The only medication they had for such a wound was a 'sulfa' pack that was supposed to stop blood poisoning.

With seven adults living close together in an 18 x 32 foot cabin, it was easy to figure out when one of the seven was missing. So it was that the youngest member of their group, Staufo, seemed to disappear many evenings without anyone's knowledge of his whereabouts. Arnest became concerned about his son's actions but Jean didn't seem worried in the least. There was no discussion about what was going on, but Jean never worried. She knew something that Arnest and the rest of the group did not.

The Simmons were constantly getting offers to sell their Morgans, but Arnest was firm about keeping his brood—after all, the family needed these horses to return to the East someday. But early in the spring four of the mares foaled, and the Simmons suddenly had three colt mares and one stallion for sale. Jean checked on horse prices carefully, and the group agreed that it was better to ask too much money for the young animals than to sell them too cheap. After all, they were short one horse already for the trip back to the East (the mare that they gave to the Paiutes in the Truckee Meadows).

So they asked $300.00 for the stallion and sold it within a week. The asked $200.00 for the mares and they sold in the next month. Suddenly they had a lot of money, but no one considered getting out of the gold-hunting busi-ness—after all, that was why the family came to the California Territory in the first place.

According to the merchants at the general store in Coloma, the level of the American River would vary from week to week, but even when the water level was low the water temperature would be so cold that a person couldn't last long in the current. According to them, the water would rise to its highest flood stage in late April, when the snows of the Sierra Nevada began to melt. Then, by middle May the water level would return to normal but the water temperature would remain close to freezing.

When the water temperature in the American River increased (after the spring run-off), the Cherokee men began replacing the troughs in the stream. By the end of May they were back in business. The general store featured a new rub-berized outfit with boots, one that a person could place his feet into and place the top of the outfit over one's shoulders, a lot like the 'coveralls' that farmers wore. The people at the general store called them 'waders'; they had been invented by a trout fisherman in England. Everyone wore cotton longjohns all the time (except when Jean called them in for washing every month or so) and the longjohns plus the water-tight waders made life on the American River bearable.

As money became more plentiful, Jean told her boys to cut enough fence posts to build a chicken coop that would hold 100 chickens. She wanted a shelter for them (from the sun, the rain, and the wind). Then she visited the wagon-works where Staufo worked and began to ask about the availability of used, lightweight wagons that could carry ten chicken coops. At first the owner of the works did not take her seriously, but after she visited two or three times, he (the owner) began to search for a buckboard for her.

Two months later he found one that was a fixer-upper, and he offered to rebuild it for Jean. Staufo had learned a lot about wagons so he took the old buckboard and added wide steel bands around the wooden wheels to improve the wagon's floatation. Having been through one rainy season, he knew how easily the narrow buckboard wheels would mire down in the mud.

Word began to come that, forty miles downstream of the Mill, in Old Sacramento City, the Sacramento River was experiencing its worst flood levels in a hundred years and most of the old city was under water. The Coloma Mill settlement people couldn't spend a lot of time worrying about Sacramento's water problems—they had flooding problems of their own.

As soon as Jean picked up her rebuilt buckboard from the wagon-works, she and We Sa went into the chicken-dressing business. The trip to the Parker farm and the return was one very long day's ride, but the days were getting longer as June approached. Bixby was bored with the gold work on the river, so he offered to make the trips to the Parker farm for chickens while Jean and We Sa dressed the chickens behind the cabin at the settlement. When Chin complained that his daughter was spending too much time dressing chickens (the Zhou family ate pretty well for a family of gold campers because We Sa was an excellent cook), Bixby was tagged to help Jean in the chicken-dressing business. He was especially good at this task, having killed and dressed thousands of beavers in the past fifty years.

✤   ✤   ✤

Jean made it a point to write to her daughters at home every three months or so. There was no Post Office close by, but by riding forty miles down the American River to Old Sacramento City she could mail a letter. The letter would arrive in Tahlequah in four to six weeks.

Her girls were instructed to write to Arnest Simmons at General Delivery in Sacramento City, so about every month or so someone in the Cherokee group would go to the Post Office and ask for Arnest's mail. They usually got one letter each time, written either by Eileen or Marcy. The letters were short, and reported mostly on everyone's health. There were never any letters from Claire. So it was not a great surprise to the California Cherokees when Marcy reported in September 1850 that Claire was having a terrible bout with fever. "Claire must have got something from one of the children in her class," Marcy wrote, "and she has been bedridden ever since. The Doctor suggested that she continue to live at her own house because what she has may be contagious. So either Eileen or myself goes to see her every day. We don't know if she is doing better or worse as the days go by—but she keeps a low fever all the time."

A month later Marcy wrote again, reporting Claire's death at the Tahlequah hospital. Jean read the letter carefully to her older brother. He remained motionless, sitting on the bench at the front door to the cabin for several minutes. As the evening progressed, each member of the group spent a few minutes with Howey to convey their condolences to him at the passing of his wife. He acknowledged their words, and sat on the bench with tears flowing down his cheeks.

Howey had never been a very 'outgoing' sort of person—he relied on Claire to maintain their contacts with their neighbors and friends. She arranged all the social events and signed up for all the annual group activities at the church, the school, and the Cherokee Nation hall. Howey would never have made it this far in life had it not been for Claire. Now she was gone, and he never even had a chance to say 'goodbye'.

Staufo mentioned later that, in the time they had been in California, Howey had written three letters to his wife. Howey always asked Staufo to mail them in Old Sacramento City, and the third letter had been mailed only a few weeks before she died. As far as the family knew, none of his letters had ever been answered by Claire. This was hard to understand because Claire had been teaching in the nearby Cherokee school for several years, and writing came easy for her.

"I hope she didn't become so sick that she couldn't write," Jean mentioned. The family had watched in dismay over the years as Claire went through one miscarriage after another. She wanted children so badly, but her body never cooperated. They were sure that Howey wanted children also, but it was not to be.

Jean decided that she was going to watch-over her older brother carefully in the next few months because he had lost what little contact he had with every-day life—Claire was his 'window to the world.'

❧   ❧   ❧

Fights continued to break out between neighbors along the river and occasionally gunshots were heard, especially in the late evening. The County Sheriff had asked that a contingent of U. S. Cavalry Troops be stationed somewhere in the Sutter Mill area to keep the peace, but the Army argued that keeping the peace there in Coloma was the Sheriff's job.

The Sheriff knew that he was going to need a new, larger jail in the near future, so he began asking the town's merchants to contribute to a fund to build the jail. He was able to get all the lumber he wanted locally for free, including oak slabs for the building foundation and ponderosa pine for the sides and roof. The general store gave him cut nails and hammers. But the one thing he did not have was a source of wrought-iron gates and the cell-bars so the prisoners could be viewed easily by the jail keeper.

Then someone in the county offices remembered that there was a young man who was a blacksmith—he had arrived recently from the East. Maybe he could make the gates and cells for the new jail. His name was Tim Wisnant.

So it was that a few days later Sheriff Rogers and his Deputy, a retired U. S. Army Cavalry Sergeant named Beavers, came to the Cherokee cabin in the evening to talk with Tim. After all the introductions were made the two men sat down at the table and explained their predicament.

Sheriff Rogers began with "Mr. Wisnant, we need a newer, bigger jail for the Village of Coloma and Eldorado County because the number of people in this county has grown from 2,000 to over 50,000 in the past two years. We have lumber donated for the project, nails, hammers, roofing, and all that, but the thing we do not have is the wrought-iron for the jail cells and the doors to the cells. The Territory of California will give me the wrought-iron to build the jail cells and they will pay for a forge to be moved from an old Army post in Los Angeles to Coloma. The forge is laying there in pieces, waiting for someone to move it. But they won't move the forge here until I guarantee them that I have a blacksmith who can do the iron work."

The Sheriff paused, and then continued, "Will you do the ironwork for us?"

Tim was slow to answer, so the Sheriff continued: "I know that you came here to mine for gold, and I know that has to be your most important thing in your mind. But this county needs a blacksmith for a few months to build the jail, and we will pay you well if you will do it."

The truth was, tending to the long-toms and sluices required that the Cherokees work long hours every day, but there was nothing exciting about the work. And they had more men in the family to do the sluicing out on the river than they really needed. Tim looked at Arnest and Arnest nodded his head up and down.

Tim began with "You can just call me 'Tim', Sheriff, which is what everyone else calls me. Yes, I will do the ironwork for you for the new jail. Go ahead and have the forge brought here to Coloma."

Tim hadn't asked what the labor rate was, but he was surprised when the Sheriff offered him $18.00 a day to do the ironwork. "That will be fine," Tim responded. It was obvious that the Sheriff was between a rock and a hard place—he had to find a blacksmith in a hurry.

CHAPTER 10

Jail Building

In the next few days Tim found himself extremely busy. Sergeant Beavers had a plan for the new jail, but there were a lot of dimensions missing. Tim got the Sheriff's Office to commit to some fixed dimensions for the jail cells, and then he was able to assign dimensions to the wrought-iron components.

"This doesn't seem to be a very big jail," Tim commented to Sergeant Beavers. "Only three cells and an emergency fire escape door at the rear. The hallway that ends at the fire door is awfully narrow."

"That's what the Sheriff wanted," Beavers explained. "Two men per cell, 10 feet by 10 feet. One pea-hole through the side of the wall per cell, and the outhouse is just outside the fire door in the rear.

Now Tim understood the real purpose of the 'fire door' at the rear of the jail.

"So the jail guard has to go with the prisoner to the outhouse?" Tim asked.

"Yep, that's the way it works," Beavers explained. "We have a shackle that we put on the prisoner's legs before we open the back door, so he can't run away."

"Then the jail guard has to put the shackle on the prisoner after he comes out of the cell?" Tim asked.

Beavers had this quizzled expression on his face. "Nope, it's not supposed to work that way."

A few seconds later Beavers added, "I'll ask the Sheriff about all that tonight."

The next day Sergeant Beavers had all the answers. "Each cell door is supposed to have two pass-throughs," he told Tim. "The one on the floor level will be one foot wide and eight inches tall. The prisoner has to stick his two feet out the front of the cell and the jail guard puts the leg irons on him."

He continued with, "The upper pass-through is also one foot wide, but only four inches tall. It starts at your waist, about thirty inches from the floor. To give a prisoner food you pass the food tray through the upper pass-through. To put handcuffs on the jail guard he sticks his hands through the upper pass-through and the jail guard puts the handcuffs on him.

Tim was writing all this down in great detail because it was time to make the cell doors at the forge.

"The locks at the front door to the jail, the back door, and the three cells will all be different locks," Beavers explained.

"Is the back door made of bars, or is it a solid door?" Tim asked.

"It's a solid wood door," Beavers said. "Both the front and back doors have to be solid; else everybody will freeze in that building in the winter. There will be a small fireplace at the front of the jail, but it won't help the people in the back very much."

Then Beavers added, "This jail is built mostly so drunks can dry-out over night. We don't plan to use the jail for thieves and murderers—only short-time visitors. We won't be using the outhouse much."

Once all that was done Tim was able to give the lady in the county offices who ordered all materials, a list of raw materials needed to do the job. When she saw the list her eyes opened wide.

"This is going to take a while to get," she told Tim. "I'll bet we can't even get some of these items in Monterrey, which means that we're going to have to go all the way to Los Angeles for them."

Indeed, Los Angeles was a long way away. Then Tim remembered that he was supposed to ask how one could get a complete forge that was sitting in an abandoned cavalry station in Los Angeles moved to Coloma. The lady explained that procuring the wrought-iron was the biggest task she had ever undertaken, and finding a way to move a forge from Los Angeles to Coloma would probably take an act of God himself. She suggested that he visit the Sheriff, who, in her words, was an "extremely ambitious person, and sometimes his schemes don't work out the way they are supposed to. But he keeps trying."

The Sheriff was determined to get the forge moved to Coloma, and he knew that the rainy season was close at hand. His appointed his Deputy, Sergeant Beavers, as the head of a committee to get the forge moved from Los Angeles to Coloma as quickly as possible. Beavers left the next day for Monterrey, which was both the U. S. Army Headquarters for the State of California and the present seat of the State of California (the Governor and both houses of the California Legislature had moved there earlier in the year, from San Jose).

Everyone was agreed that the forge should be moved, but no one would pay for the shipment. So Beavers, whose frustration was reaching epic proportions, placed a 'poke' of gold onto the desk of the Commanding General of the U. S. Army in California and told him, "Here is the money to ship the forge to Coloma. If you don't have the forge in Coloma by two months from now then I will personally petition the governor of this state to have your offices moved to a town ten miles south of San Diego, on the Mexican border. If you want to keep your job here, then move the forge to Coloma."

The General said nothing, but inside he was smoking mad. After some more gentle talk, Beavers left his office. Monterrey was clearly the most desirable city in California to live in, and the General liked it there. He wasn't sure how much clout Sergeant Beavers had with the Governor of California, but he didn't want to take any chances. Six weeks later the disassembled forge arrived in Coloma, but the rainy season had already started. It turned out that the lady who gave Beavers the gold to ship the forge was the owner of the biggest saloon in

Coloma. Apparently she was ready for a new jail to be built—some of her customers needed a place to 'dry out' after an evening of entertainment at her saloon. Her name was Sally Jo Timmons.

The next week, Tim reminded Beavers that a forge took more heat than pine lumber could deliver, so someone had to find hardwood for the forge. Sergeant Beavers asked if 'scrub oak' was acceptable as firewood.

"You bet," Tim replied. "But we're goin' to need a lot of it. We can burn a cord of hardwood every three days on the forge."

Beavers was pleased. "Good," Beavers replied, "because I know where there is lots of scrub oak, all on state land, and we have the authority to use it. The county owns a wagon with a team of draft horses that can tote a cord of wood at a time.

Then Beavers added: "While we're hauling lumber I want to bring a lot of firewood to the county offices on Main Street—we nearly froze to death last winter.

Arnest and Howey got into the jail-building discussion when they reminded the Sheriff that the proposed location for the new jail was barely above the river high-water level in the summer and fall, and it would flood every spring. Since the foundation for the building was already in place, Sergeant Beavers, Arnest, Howey, and Tim figured out a way to raise the main floor by four feet. To do this, Beavers and the Sheriff had to procure some hefty planking that was not included in the original plan for the building and no one would give them any more money to build the jail.

So Renwe brought his boss to the site (from the sawmill) and a plan was hatched to get the lumber from a nearby stand of oak trees. To procure the trees, the Sheriff convinced the Mayor of Coloma that the oak tree site would be perfect for the new school that the settlement was talking about, and a sawmill would do the tree removal for free (to show their spirit of cooperation in the affairs of the city).

Taking the oak trees to a saw mill near Hangtown was a real chore, so Sergeant Beavers contacted Colonel Sutter in Sacramento and asked for permission to saw the lumber at his new sawmill (the one that had yet to produce its first piece of sawed wood for sale). The Colonel immediately agreed, and the new lumber was ready for emplacement at the jail site in four weeks.

Tim found that it was practically impossible to create door keys and locks on such a primitive forge, so the owner of the big general store in Coloma found a place in Connecticut that made precision cast iron locks and keys. This was the same company that made forgings for the Colt revolver company. He ordered the locks and keys; they were slow to arrive because they were sent by ship from Boston, all the way around the end of South America. It took six months for the locks and keys to arrive.

By October 1850 the jail was complete except for the locks and the keys. The forge had been set-up on a small hill overlooking the jail and the original county land-deed building. Tim was able to forge all the ironwork as fast as the building could be built, and he was paid well by the county. The forge area was open to the sun and rain but the Sheriff promised that he would have a roof on it soon.

The next March the keys and locks arrived in Coloma and the jail was completed. The manufacturer had thrown some extra keys into the package from Boston, so some of the locks had two matching keys and some had three matching keys. Beavers kept all the extra keys and stored them at his house.

On the one-year anniversary of the event when the Cherokees took over the gold-hunting tasks from the O'Leary family (in November 1849), the Cherokees declared a holiday to celebrate their good fortune in coming to California. Thanksgiving was only a couple of weeks away. The Zhou family was invited to a long afternoon of eating and drinking and they all came. Fortunately, from the Simmons cabin one could observe the entire Zhou and O'Leary placers, so there was no need to guard the gold camp one hundred percent of the time.

During the festivities, Chin spoke at great length with Arnest and Jean about his problems with his youngest son, Yang. Chin needed some advice on what to do with the young man, who had become a womanizer in the settlement and consumed ever-increasing amounts of liquor. Yang was a tall, good look-ing Chinese with dimples on his cheeks and dark black hair. He knew how to talk to the ladies at the local bars and he spent many evenings there looking for a suitable woman to spend an evening with.

Chin was frantic because none of his other sons ever acted like Yang did. Chin knew that the young white men in these bars despised the Chinese, and his son was making a lot of enemies in the settlement. If Chin had his way, he would send Yang back to the Nebraska Territory right now, but there was no way to do that. The family had decided that in one year they would return to Nebraska anyway, for lots of reasons: Yang's continuing problems with liquor and with the neighbors, the decrease in the amount of gold being taken from the river every month, and the fact that the family had more than enough gold to buy desirable farm land near New Fort Kearney (which was the whole purpose of the trip to the California gold country).

This was the first time the two men had discussed Fort Kearney and Nebraska. Arnest mentioned that he had been lead to believe that Chin's family was from San Francisco. Chin laughed, and explained: "Soon after we got to Sutter's Mill we were asked if we were part of the Zhou family of San Francisco. I didn't know what to say, but I know that my family never immigrated to San Francisco—they came to America from Paris, France, where they were indentured to a wealthy silk merchant from Hong Kong named Ne Yan. He treated the Zhou family well, and had them maintain a residence for him northwest of Washington, DC, in a town named Bethesda. When the oldest son, Hi Te Yan, finished his education he decided to sell silk in St. Louis, and some of my family went with him to establish a residence there."

"There was no 'indenturing' by this time—my family went with Hi Te because he was the smartest person in the family, and my father knew that he would do well no matter where he would go. My wife and I were both born in St. Louis, and we both attended school there. Her family lived only a few blocks away from our house on Center Street. After we were married we wanted to go in business for ourselves, so Hi Te arranged for us to go with a military group that was going to build the original Fort Kearney on the Missouri River. General Kearney was the big hero of the Mexican War, you know."

He continued with: "No sooner was the fort on the Missouri River built when the Army decided to tear it down and build a new Fort Kearney on the North Platte River. We did a lot of work for the commander there after the new fort was built, and my wife established a trading post near the front gate. The reason she did not come with us to California is that her business interests in the Nebraska Territory were taking all her time."

Arnest was learning a lot. After a pause, Chin continued: "My children speak French, American, and a dialect of Chinese. So you can imagine how angry the young white men in the 'Lone Star of Texas' Saloon become when he answers their taunts by speaking to them in French. He thinks it is funny to respond to them in this way, but I fear for his safety in situations like that."

After this discussion, Arnest wondered how things were going with his two sons and his 'ward', Tim Wisnant. So he and Jean approached each one individually, in the evening, away from the cabin, asking what their future plans were. There was no reason to assume that these young men were happy with the plans that the Simmons family had made. Maybe they didn't want to return to the Kansas Territory, or Tahlequah. Maybe California was becoming their home.

They were not surprised that the young men were totally noncommittal about their future plans. For one thing, none of them had serious girlfriends back home or the Kansas Territory. Arnest never got a straight reply from Staufo about what his son was doing on those evenings when he disappeared for several hours at a time. What was all that about?

Arnest asked Jean if she knew anything about Staufo's disappearances, and Jean walked with him to the chicken coops to talk privately. Then Jean told him about the budding romance between Staufo and We Sa, the little Chinese girl who was growing up before their very eyes. Now Arnest was beginning to understand some things.

❧   ❧   ❧

This year the rains came later than usual, so the Cherokee group was unable to 'sluice' for gold until much later in the season. Their monthly visitor, Hubert O'Leary, was pleased with the year 1850 in terms of the amount of gold taken from the American River, and he said so. But he also had the feeling that 1851 would not be as good as 1850. "Do you think this river is about mined-out?" Hubert asked Arnest and Chin.

"It's hard to say," Chin responded. "We hear about big gold finds up the river and big gold finds farther down the river. We even hear about gold in the Sacramento River itself. The Mariposa is supposed to be bringing in more gold than we do here, also. But you can't prove that any of these rumors are true."

Arnest joined the discussion: "If your figures are correct for all the gold you took out of this river a year ago, then we are definitely depleting the gold source. But all that we are mining is the gold that continues to come down the river. It could be that we're sitting right on top of the biggest gold find of them all—the gold deep in the riverbed. This river may have been carrying gold down from the mountains for thousands of years, and the riverbed continues to build-up higher and higher to cover that gold."

"But there's no way we can 'mine' the riverbed without routing the river around our claims—and that sounds like something that takes a lot of time and a lot of money," Chin added.

"Is there anything we can do to look at the first couple feet of riverbed, to see if it has a lot of gold in it?" Hubert asked.

Arnest and Chin had to think about that. They promised to devise a way to look at the sand and fill below the riverbed to see if it contained gold.

There were no newspapers in the Sutter Mill area, so Hubert was their only source of information about what was going on around the world. As he was leaving the campsite, he told Renwe and Staufo that he was going to move to southern California in the next year to go to law school. His younger brother, Winston, would assume the duties of 'agent' for the O'Leary family and would make his first visit in May of 1851 (six months from now) because there would be so little gold hunting activity until next spring.

Since the Cherokee group had been in the gold-hunting business for over a year, Jean and Arnest decided to gather some information about how well the group was doing financially. To spend money in the Cherokee group it was necessary that the spender take an amount of gold dust out of one of the four leather pokes that were situated at various places in the cabin and purchase the items. It was a terrible money-handling system but there was no alternative.

The general store had started making change using American silver dollars, fifty-cent pieces, quarters, dimes, and pennies. They also had a few five-dollar and twenty-dollar gold pieces that were minted in Philadelphia, but they seldom put them back into circulation. So the principal medium of exchange continued to be 'gold dust'.

The general store owner preferred to take whatever gold was contained in a customer's poke, weigh it, and credit the customer with that much money ($19.73 per troy ounce). Then they subtracted every item purchased from that total until the account went negative. Now the customer was expected to hand over another poke of gold. The only advantage for the customer was that he or she could get in and out of the store in a hurry since there was no meticulous 'weighing' of the gold that the customer offered every time an item was purchased. With the old 'pay as you go' scheme, making the payment at the end of the session at the store took more time than collecting the items in the store to be purchased because gold-weighing was such a slow process.

The merchants were the most concerned about being handed a poke that was supposed to be gold, but was really part gold and part filler. The favorite 'filler' for some of the more unsavory customers was a black granular compound that contained almost pure silver. But silver was only worth one sixth what gold was worth (but it was just as heavy).

Later on, the general store offered a small discount for those who 'paid in advance', since this gave the merchant the opportunity to check the contents of a poke very carefully.

At the Cherokee cabin, the decision had already been made by the group that the total monies in these gold pokes would be divided up equally by all members of the group (7 people) when the group returned East.

There was an ongoing discussion in the cabin about whether it was better to 'sluice' for gold all the time in the American River or go some place close and work for someone else. Tim had made an incredible amount of money while the jail was being built, but that was all finished now. Some months Renwe and Staufo brought home the most money just by working at the sawmill and the wagon-works. Other months the 'sluicing' brought in the most money. The chicken-dressing work brought in less money than the sawmill and the wagon-works and the sluicing, but Jean and We Sa could only work that job 40 hours a week—everyone else worked a 60 hour a week job. The rest of the time Jean and We Sa did all the cooking and clothes washing.

The merchants and shops in the area had a continuing need for clerks, and the price for these clerks was going up regularly. In 1850 the standard rate was $6.00 a day. The standard day was ten hours long, and most workers were expected to work six days a week. Everything was shut down on Sundays except the liquor stores and the two bars. Both Staufo and Renwe were bringing home $8.00 a day. In San Francisco the standard rate for retail clerks was still one to two dollars a day, but San Francisco labor rates were catching up with goldfield labor rates because of supply and demand (all the young people in San Francisco were leaving their jobs and coming to the Sutter Mill or the Mariposa to search for gold).

Jean and We Sa's chicken dressing business had brought in profits of $7.00 a day for each (after they paid for the buckboard). They were open for chicken sales four days a week. The one-dollar chicken was now a $1.25 chicken. But they had some stiff competition from a group in Coloma and might have to reduce the price back to $1.00 in 1851.

The gold sluicing was bringing in about $20.00 a day per person on the placers (Arnest, Howey, Tim, and Bixby) (6 day week) but half of that went to the O'Leary family. So the group who was making the least amount of money in the family over the entire year were the four men who tended the sluices (they could only mine for gold seven months out of the year). They were not about to stop sluicing for gold however since the posted price for 'laborers' at such far away places as San Diego or Yuma was only 1 dollar a day—'Sluicing' was still their best money-maker.

The Cherokees knew how to keep their expenses down. Tim and Bixby took small amounts of gold out of the leather pokes to meet their tobacco and alcohol cravings (since it was known that Renwe and Staufo kept monies back from the family to support their free-time activities). By Arnest and Jean's calculations, after paying all their expenses, at the end of the first year, the group had amassed a gold fortune of about $12,000.00. Split seven ways, this was $1714.00 per person. A full section of land along the South Platte River (640 acres) in the Kansas Territory would cost $1920.00 ($3 per acre).

At this point in time there was no reason to stop doing what they were doing.

CHAPTER 11

The Coloma Gentry

Jean and We Sa had a great chicken-dressing business going. The distance from the Simmons cabin to the middle of downtown Coloma was only 300 yards. People in Coloma would send their youngsters over to the Simmons cabin with cash in hand to bring dressed chickens home. Some of the more permanent (and well-to-do) families in Coloma drove their buckboards over to Jean's house to pick up dressed chickens because there were low spots along the edge of the river where their kids picked up lots of mud on their shoes and clothes.

The Sheriff's wife, Lee Ann Rogers, was one of Jean's and We Sa's best customers. She owned the biggest hotel in town and a lot of people ate in the main dining room on the weekends. She bought so many dressed chickens that she finally worked out a plan with Jean that saved her from coming to the cabin on Fridays—she got Bixby to deliver the correct number of chickens on Friday afternoon about two hours before the evening meal was served. This number grew in leaps and bounds until it was 50 or so every weekend. Lee Ann finally built an ice house to keep the chickens fresher longer.

Jean and We Sa had another customer who bought fewer chickens, but she insisted on picking out every chicken herself. He name was Sally Jo Timmons; she was the owner of the biggest saloon in town. Lee Ann and Sally Jo did not see eye-to-eye on a lot of important issues, but they were both smart enough to keep their differences out of their day-to-day dealings.

Sheriff Rogers had been the County Sheriff for over ten years, and he wanted to continue to serve in that office for at least another ten years. So he never hassled Sally Jo Timmons, who was the town's biggest cheerleader, philanthropist, and madam.

Sally Jo rode in the county's only 'Surrey With the Fringe On Top'. She had a full-time driver named Herman who took her everywhere she went. When Sally Jo would come to the Simmons cabin and pick out a dozen chickens or so ('for some of the boys at the saloon' she would always say), she always had Herman drive her back to the saloon immediately, and he would come back later to pick up the freshly-dressed Rhode Island Reds.

One day, when she seemed to have more time to talk than she usually did, she struck up a conversation with Arnest about how things were going in the gold-sluicing business. "I never did get into the gold-panning business," she told Arnest, Jean, and We Sa while they were dressing her chickens. "I came to Coloma about five years ago to open a hotel here, and then I found out that this town had more hotels than it had people."

Arnest asked her where she lived before she came to Coloma. "My husband and I were in South Dakota" she responded. "After he died I sold the business near Rapid City and moved out here."

She didn't mention what her business was in Rapid City, so We Sa asked her. "We had a saloon," she said. "It was small—nothing near as big as what I have here in Coloma. But we made money—there were lots of thirsty miners in South Dakota at the time."

As she and Hermann prepared to leave, she asked where Mr. Zhou's claim was, and Jean pointed it out to her. "It's only 200 yards from here," Jean explained, "it's on the river and it has a red, white, and blue flag flying from their main tent."

Sally Jo thanked them for the information and she and Herman made their way to the Zhou tents.

"I sure would like to be in on that conversation," Arnest mentioned that evening. "Yang spends more and more time at Sally Jo's saloon—I wonder if Yang owes her money."

Chin made no mention of Sally Jo's visit to their claim so Arnest couldn't bring up the topic. Arnest asked Renwe and Staufo if they knew anything about Yang's dealings at the saloon, but they only shook their heads and claimed to know nothing. Obviously if they knew anything about events at the saloon they would never admit it to their father and mother.

CHAPTER 12

A Grand Experiment

Both Arnest and Chin felt like they should answer Hubert O'Leary's question that he had posed some two months earlier: "Is there significant gold in the riverbed of the American River where the Zhou and O'Leary claims are located?

If there was no river present, this would be an easy experiment to conduct. You could mark off a small area (maybe four feet by four feet) and dig down a couple feet of so to see what the riverbed contained in the way of precious metals.

But how do you stop the river? At no time did the river ever stop flowing. There was a lot more water flowing in the spring than there was in the winter, but the river never stopped completely. Or did it?

"A hundred years from now someone will have all this figured out," Howey mentioned at the dinner table one evening. "We're just too far ahead of our time."

Tim decided that he was going to pose that question to the Sheriff, because the Sheriff had lived in Eldorado County all his life. His Deputy, Sergeant Beavers, was a newcomer to the county so he wouldn't know much about that.

But when Tim talked to Beavers, Beavers had a suggestion about who might know the answer to what was in the riverbed—Mr. Marshall himself. Marshall had built the sawmill for Sutter and he planned the complete excavation of the area around the mill. That seemed like an incredibly good idea, so the first time Tim had a free Sunday he convinced Bixby that they should visit Mr. Marshall. "They tell me that he only lives about ten miles from here," Tim told Bixby. "And they say that he seldom goes anywhere—he is a bit of a hermit. We could get directions to his cabin from someone in the Sheriff's office and ride the Morgan horses up there for a visit."

"What if Mr. Marshall loads up his shotgun with rock salt and blasts us off his property?" Bixby asked.

"What makes you think he would do a thing like that?" Tim asked.

"You said he was kind of a 'hermit', and hermits sometimes do strange things," Bixby responded.

Tim was trying to think ahead of Bixby: "What if we ask the Sheriff to go with us and introduce us to Mr. Marshall? After all, we built a jail for him last year. He may want to repay the favor."

Bixby had to think about that. "All right," he said, "let's go talk to the Sheriff."

"Today is Sunday," Tim reminded Bixby.

"Then we'll go over to his wife's hotel and talk to him there," Bixby suggested.

So the two men put on their Sunday best and walked up to the hotel. When they got there they asked if the Sheriff was there and the Maitre D' told them that the Sheriff was helping in the kitchen. "Don't get him all tied-up with your problems," the Maitre D' told them, "because his job is to taste everything and make sure it is all right to serve to the guests."

When they entered the kitchen they saw the Sheriff immediately—he was seated at a small wooden chopping block with small plates of food all around him. The Sheriff invited them to sit down with him, so they did.

Tim lead the conversation: "Sheriff," he said, "we need to figure out a way to visit Mr. Marshall because we have some questions we would like to ask him.

But we don't know where he lives, and we don't know if he would let us into his cabin if we just went there and knocked on his door. Can you help us?"

The Sheriff thought for a moment, picked up one of the main courses for the day, ate it, wiped his lips with a linen napkin, and pushed back from the table. "He is a difficult person to talk to because he travels around the county a lot—alone. He also makes frequent trips to Sacramento because he and his old employer, Colonel Sutter, seem to have a lot to talk about."

"Maybe the Colonel owes him some money."

There was a pause—the Sheriff was thinking. "The best way to meet him and talk with him is to get him to come here to Coloma, and I'll bet I can arrange that! If I go to all this trouble to get him to come to Coloma, I hope your questions are worth asking."

"We would be much obliged if you could do a thing like that," Bixby said.

The Sheriff thought some more, than made this suggestion: "Let's pick a Sunday at least two weeks from now, about 1 o'clock in the afternoon, and we'll set up a private dining room on the second floor. The hotel will prepare a simple meal because he won't eat fancy food. We'll serve steaks, some kind of special potatoes with cheese mixed in, and fried okra. My wife and I will attend, and all your family can come, but that's all we can fit into those upstairs dining rooms."

"Fried okra?" Bixby asked.

"So far as I know, that's the only vegetable that he will eat," the Sheriff replied. "What's the matter, Bixby, don't you like fried okra?"

"Oh yessir, yessir, I love fried okra," Bixby replied. The truth was, Bixby had never eaten okra in his life. He didn't even know what it looked like.

"Then let's consider it done!" the Sheriff announced.

He paused for a moment, then added: "I'll have to get my wife to agree to all this. She owns this hotel, you know."

❧   ❧   ❧

When Tim announced to the Simmons group that they were all invited to meet Mr. Marshall, the designer and builder of the Sutter sawmill, there was some excitement in the cabin. "Is he the one who found the first gold nuggets?" Staufo asked.

"Yes, he was," Bixby replied. "The Mormon Battalion was finishing up the tail-race below the undershot waterwheel when he found small nuggets of gold."

Jean was not particularly excited about going to meet Mr. Marshall when she found out that they had to go to the Rogers' hotel on Main Street. No one in the family had ever set foot in that building. "We are probably expected to dress-up nicely for such an event, and I didn't bring any kind of a dress to California except the ones I wear around the cabin. I don't even know where to go to buy a new dress."

We Sa agreed to watch-over the cabin while the Simmons were gone to meet Mr. Marshall, and she had a solution for Jean's new dress problem: "Why don't you ask Sally Jo Timmons to go with you to pick out a new dress that you can wear to the dinner?" We Sa suggested.

Everyone thought that was a wonderful idea, except for Jean. "Sally Jo Timmons wears the most exclusive, most expensive clothes in this county. If she takes me to a boutique in Hangtown or Sacramento it will cost me an arm and a leg for a dress!" she exclaimed.

There was a pause, and then Renwe entered the discussion: "Mom, you been working awfully hard for the past year—you deserve to go to a fine dinner in a fine dress, and you know it."

Jean was trying to come up with a counter-plan. She turned to Arnest and asked him, "If I get all dressed up for this event, Arnest, what are you going to wear, since you will be my escort?"

Arnest was not prepared for this question. He looked to the left, then to the right, and remained silent for several seconds. Then his face brightened-up when he announced, "I'll buy a pair of black dress pants, a white shirt, and a string tie, that's what I'll do."

So the attire for the event was settled—at least for Jean and Arnest. In the next few days Tim, Bixby, Renwe, and Staufo all realized that they had to follow Arnest's example, and they too had to purchase new outfits for this event. "If I had realized what we were getting ourselves into," Bixby declared, "I would never have opened my mouth about visiting with Mr. Marshall."

Later in the week the Simmons all knew that the event was firmly on the family schedule because Lee Ann Rogers sent them a written invitation by special messenger—one of the busboys at the hotel.

Meanwhile, Jean finally got her nerve up enough to visit the Lone Star of Texas Saloon where Sally Jo Timmons lived, and she and Sally talked about procuring a dress for this big event. "Before we go off to Sacramento or Monterrey, let me show you what is available right here in Coloma," Sally suggested. "There are two seamstresses here in town who can put a dress together in a week, if needs be."

Then Sally Jo showed Jean what the Timmons wardrobe looked like and Jean picked one out that suited her fancy. Sally Jo spoke with her driver, Herman, and asked him to check to see if the seamstresses were in town this week, so off he went. An hour later Herman returned with the good news that the Far d'Loure sisters were available, and would Sally Jo and Jean please come to their place of business in one hour.

"I never heard about these seamstresses," Jean mentioned. "I guess there are more people living in this community than I know about."

Sally Jo explained that they had come to Coloma from South Dakota, not too long after Sally Jo moved to Coloma. "I wrote them a letter," Sally Jo explained, "and told them that their services were needed badly in this charming little Mexican community."

By late that evening, Jean had been measured for her new dress and was scheduled for a first-fitting in three days. Jean was puzzled at how two sisters could produce such a dress in that short of a time. "Maybe they run to Monterrey and steal dresses there," Arnest suggested. If only he knew how close he was to being right.

When Jean received the dress a week later she asked for the bill, and was told that the total price was thirty dollars. She paid the delivery man the money and then began to ask him some questions about the dress. But the delivery man claimed to know nothing about the dress except that the Far d'Loure sisters had handed it to him to be delivered to the Simmons cabin.

After the delivery man left, Jean tried the dress on, and it fit perfectly. The dress was accompanied by a shawl, a headpiece, and dress shoes with sparkles all over the leather. "There is something very deceptive here," Jean announced to her husband. "No one makes a dress like this for thirty dollars, much less one with all the accessories that accompanied this dress. The material alone in this dress costs a whole lot more than thirty dollars. What is going on?"

Arnest just shrugged his shoulders in a typical husband fashion.

❧   ❧   ❧

On the appointed Sunday afternoon the Simmons entourage arrived at the Rogers' Hotel at 1 p.m. Sally Jo Timmons had arranged for Arnest and Jean to be transported to the hotel in her one-horse surrey, driven by Herman. "You will never make it through the mud at the edge of the river in those dancing shoes," Sally Jo told Jean.

They were met by Lee Ann and Rupert Rogers at the front steps to the hotel, and were escorted to a small dining room on the second floor. Inside the dining room they were introduced to the venerable 'Mr. James Marshall', the now-famous builder of the Sutter Mill.

The Mayor of Coloma and his wife were also present, as was the presiding judge of the county court. Cocktails were served, both alcoholic and non-alcoholic, since it was generally known that Arnest and Jean were teetotalers. The main course was served shortly thereafter, as was the salad course, and finally the dessert. After the dessert, cigars were placed at the right-side of each gentleman, and they were encouraged to light-up immediately.

Sheriff Rogers stood up and introduced James Marshall, the 'man who started all this confusion in Eldorado County'. Marshall rose, and spoke for a few minutes about how he happened to come to Coloma in 1848 (Colonel Sutter had hired him to build a sawmill on the American River). He was asked questions about how he chose the site for the sawmill, and if he had it to do all over again, would he have built the sawmill somewhere else.

"I don't think so," Marshall replied. "We knew that we needed some minimum amount of water beating up against the undershot water wheel with some minimum flow rate, and that was available most anywhere along the river. The reason we built the sawmill in Coloma was because the ponderosa pine that the Colonel wanted to cut was close by."

"Was the Colonel planning to start-up the mill soon?"

"You would have to ask him," Marshall replied. "But it's very difficult to keep hired-help these days, and the Colonel will probably wait until this 'gold fever' dies down a bit before he re-opens the mill."

He continued with: "Before we re-open the mill we have to find a way to bring more water through the main spillway at the waterwheel. We may have to put more 'paddles' on the wheel and increase the height of the paddles to get enough power to run the mill. We know that there is enough water flowing through the sluice to run the mill in the springtime during the runoff, but you can't operate a sawmill that only works three months out of the year."

"How come you are using a vertical saw blade instead of a circular saw blade?"

"The vertical saw blade takes less power, and we knew that 'power' was going to be a problem. If power continues to be a problem, we may cut a new steel vertical blade that has smaller teeth on it. The larger the teeth, the more power is required to pull it through a log."

Bixby and Tim didn't ask their big question at this time. Lee Ann Rogers suggested that she show the hotel facilities to the ladies present, and 'the men can smoke in the dining room'. These were the first true Cuban cigars that Bixby and Tim had seen in a couple of years, and they planned to sit back in their chairs and enjoy the occasion.

Finally, Tim realized that the session was about to end, and he had not asked Mr. Marshall about the possibility of more gold below the surface of the river-bed. So he spoke up quickly: "Mr. Marshall," Tim asked, "is it possible that there is a lot more gold below the riverbed, gold put there thousands of years ago?"

Marshall looked directly at Tim and replied, "I think not, Sir. There was a hush-hush experiment conducted at the Mariposa gold site south of here a year ago, and the river there was completely re-routed for about six months. Laborers were brought in from San Francisco to dig up the riverbed and search for gold. They dug as deep as twenty feet in some cases, and they found very little precious metals."

Sheriff Rogers interrupted at this point, saying, "James, you better tell them the whole story. The edges of the river in the Mariposa, where the water runs deep, seem to contain significant gold at selected spots along the river. That's why a lot of companies are trying to buy-up the claims there and convert them all to hydraulic mining. The problem with hydraulic mining is that it destroys the riverbank completely. Once the gold miners leave an area that has been 'hydraulically mined' there is nothing left for future generations."

Now the question posed by Hubert O'Leary had been fully answered.

CHAPTER 13

The Second Year

In 1851 the spring floods came even later than they had in 1850, and it wasn't possible to re-set the long-toms and sluices in the river before early June. The number of new people coming into the valley around Sutter's Mill decreased because the placers that were left to distribute by Eldorado County to newcomers were located in remote parts of the rivers, high on the steppes of the Sierra Nevada Mountains. Some would have argued that these were the best places to find significant gold deposits, but it didn't work out that way. Apparently the water moved through these high steppes so quickly that very little gold was deposited there.

There were a half-a-dozen companies that set up businesses in the Sacramento and Hangtown areas for the sole purpose of buying old placers. The placers in the river or close to the river around Sutter's Mill brought about $500 apiece, but the more distant placers sold for under $100 (at a time when a good horse brought $200). The companies had brought in machinery for 'hydraulic mining', and men with high pressure hoses blasted away the sand and soft materials on the streambed and the riverbank to uncover the heavy elements left behind (gold nuggets). The process was too harsh for recovery of small flakes of gold (the kind that the Indians and Mexicans picked out of the slurry in the bottom of a trough). There were some huge gold nuggets found, but there were also a lot of miners who found nothing.

In June 1851 the hydraulic mining commenced upstream of the Mill. Soon, the river at the Mill became a dirty wash. The hydraulic miners were releasing one-hundred times as much silt and sand into the stream as was there before. Now, a miner standing in the middle of the stream below the Mill couldn't see the river bottom.

The Mormon Battalion that had occupied 'Mormon Island' was in the process of breaking up, and the men were returning to the Utah Territory. Some of them hadn't seen their family in over four years. All of their claims were purchased by mining companies from Hangtown or Sacramento.

Jean and We Sa's chicken-dressing business continued, but they had to sell the chickens at a price slightly below $1.00. There was too much competition to make significant money in the business any more. The sawmill business was still running full-speed-ahead for Renwe but the wagon-works (Staufo) had cut way back on its production of new wagons. They mostly repaired old wagons. Both Simmons boys were employed full time, but their owners weren't hiring additional employees.

As the year progressed the amount of gold brought in by the sluices on the O'Leary placer began to drop off and both Arnest and Jean could see the handwriting on the wall. Also, a family living in a cabin only 300 yards downstream of the Cherokees was attacked by a group who rushed into their cabin early one morning, tied-up the family, and killed them. The attackers used no guns—only knives, so the people around them didn't even know that a crime was being committed. The attackers searched for the family's gold as long as they could, then disappeared when the sun came up.

But the worst incident, so far as the Simmons and the Zhou's were concerned, occurred late one evening when Yang Zhou was surprised at a small bridge coming out of Coloma, was beaten-up badly, and murdered. The killers took his weapons, his gold, and even his brass belt buckle. The Sheriff's Office was becoming accustomed to handling murder investigations now—this was the third murder this year.

Sergeant Beavers visited the Cherokee cabin every month or so because he had found a friend in Tim Wisnant. Both men were unmarried and they loved the outdoors. But this time he was visiting because he wanted to know if there was anything that could be done for their neighbors, the Zhou family, after Yang's death.

"I really have to feel sorry for the Zhou family," Beavers said during his visit. "Their son was killed and we can't find anyone who admits to seeing anything that night. The bridge that he was crossing is used by every person in the settlement—it's the only way to get to the saloons, the stores, the brothels, you name it. There had to be someone who saw this big fight going on."

"I can tell you what Chin Zhou thinks about the investigation," Tim responded.

"What does he think?" Beavers asked.

"He thinks that the Sheriff's Department is not working very hard to find Yang's murderers because Yang was a Chinese," Tim responded.

"But that's not true!" Beavers said, emphatically. "We have done everything in our power to bring the murderers to justice!"

Tim thought for a while, and then commented, "I guess the last three murders we have had in the settlement will never be solved, even in the case of our neighbors down the river who were killed while they slept in their cabin. Unfortunately they were also Chinese."

"The Sheriff is at wit's end about these murders," Beavers said. "He has been the Sheriff for over ten years now, and in the first seven years there was no one killed in this county in anger. Now, in the past three years there have been seven murders in the county, and only three of those murders have been solved."

Then Beavers added, "The leaders of the Chinese here in Coloma say that they may move away and establish their own community. Only then can they protect their children."

"Have any of the Indians in the settlement been attacked?" Tim asked.

"Two of the unsolved murders involve Indians," Beavers answered. "It looks like the Indians and the Mexicans are all packing up and leaving Coloma and the county, and I can't say as I blame them. They made a living here before gold was discovered, and they can make a living after the gold is all gone, but they have to wait for the white man to clear out."

It occurred to Tim that he better make mention to Arnest that 'all the Indians were leaving'. After all, the Cherokees were Indians.

Yang's funeral was held at a small Community church on the edge of Coloma, and he was buried in the church's graveyard close to the river. Both the Sheriff and Sergeant Beavers attended the funeral, as did most of the miners and families living close to the Zhou claim.

Chin took Yang's death very personally, insisting that none of this would have happened if he hadn't forced his family to come to California to hunt for gold. Ho and Kim did their best to comfort their father, and they continued to speak of Yang's death as an act of 'fate'—kismet. They said that Yang had adopted a pattern of behavior that led to confrontation with the young white men in the settlement—the gunslingers, and when the confrontation came he was not prepared for it.

We Sa remained silent throughout the funeral, but Jean spent a lot of time with her. They walked through the forest behind the cabin and talked about many things. We Sa was not a stoic—she did not believe that a person was foreordained to have good things happen to them in life or bad things, either. Life was a mix of the good and the bad. She wanted to put all of this behind her as quickly as possible.

After one of these walks, Arnest and Jean sat by the edge of the river as the sun was going down and discussed what was happening around them. Arnest opened the conversation with "We Sa seems to be taking her brother's death as well as could be expected, and she is already returning to her old self."

Jean nodded in agreement. "She has told me lots of times that her favorite brother is Ho, because Ho is a gentle person and he looks out for the welfare of all the Zhou family. Ho insists that We Sa is the re-creation of his mother, Mi Yan, who is back at New Fort Kearney. We Sa has the same spirit and enthusiasm as her mother, and she accepts life's downturns with a minimum of grief and tears. Ho also says that she expects to do great things in this life, and if her family makes lots of money in Sutter Mill gold than she expects to further her education. She wants to teach at a university some day."

"Does she speak as many languages as her father?" Arnest asked.

"I think she speaks more languages than he does," was the reply. "Some families don't think very highly of their own women—for example, we never suggested to our girls, Eileen and Marcy, that they should continue their education and teach school or something like that. As soon as they came breathlessly into our kitchen at home and announced that a Cherokee brave had proposed marriage to them, we agreed that this was the best thing to do. Our girls may do something significant in this life, but it won't be because we guided them in that direction."

Arnest thought for a moment, and then agreed with Jean's statement. "Does Staufo go over to We Sa's tent in the evening like he used to?" Arnest asked.

Jean laughed. "All the time, Arnest, all the time. But you usually fall asleep before he returns."

"They are serious about each-other, then?"

"As serious as two people can be when they are caught-up in a whirlwind of family responsibilities. They work ten to twelve hours a day, six days a week, and Staufo travels a long distance to work. When he gets home he looks like death warmed-over, yet he eats a quick supper and is out the door by dark."

Then Jean added, "Maybe we have forgotten about the passion that a twenty-year-old can generate in his life—we were the same way thirty years ago."

"Indeed we were," Arnest returned. "Indeed we were."

There was only one funeral parlor in Coloma, and the owner had subsisted on a meager business for years. But now, when the local population increased by a factor of fifty in just three years, business was pretty good. People were dying for a lot of different reasons. There were construction accidents, especially on the creeks upstream of the Sutter Mill where the American River dropped quickly out of the Sierra Nevada Mountains. There were no antibiotics (just iodine and sulfa packs for wounds, and patent medicines for coughs and colds) and splints for broken bones. There were hunting accidents and people falling off heavy machinery. There were people being trampled by dray horses pulling large wagons, and delivery vehicles with lumber, roofing, tools, nails, tarpaper, and shingles.

Since food prices were rising so rapidly, some of the mining families planted crops around their cabins and tents—crops like corn, potatoes, radishes, and tomatoes. Chicken coops became more common, and there were even a few nanny goats who roamed the settlement regularly. "Would you believe it," Sergeant Beavers mentioned to Tim one day, "the judge has a case on his docket today to sentence two goat thieves. They claim they had to steal a goat because their children were not able to drink regular cow's milk."

No one was in charge of public sanitation, so it was a sure bet that some form of typhoid or smallpox would rear its ugly head in the settlement, and 1851 was the year. By 1852 the death rate from both typhoid and smallpox reached epidemic proportions.

When Winston O'Leary showed up in July to collect the month's gold take he was openly angry to see how little gold had been collected. Arnest and Jean assured him that this was all the gold there was, and the men were spending every daylight hour on the sluices. Winston left the Simmons's cabin and spent part of the day with Chin Zhou. Only when Chin confirmed that the amount of gold being taken from the river was decreasing, would Winston accept the monthly amount offered by Arnest. As Winston was leaving the premises, Arnest mentioned that this might be the last year that the Cherokees gold mined—the price of survival in the settlement was getting too high.

In September the Zhou family confronted misfortune again, but this time it was in the form of a legal setback. It happened this way: Late one evening, about an hour after sunset, the Simmons heard weapons being fired at the Zhou placers, so they grabbed up their handguns and rushed over to the site. They found a group of seven white men armed with handguns and rifles, and in the middle of the placers there was a large bonfire burning. The Zhou family was sitting next to the fire; each member of the family was bound with rope.

Arnest rushed to the side of Chin to ask him what was going on. Chin told him that the white men had rushed into their tents during the evening meal and tied-up everyone with rope. The leader of the group claimed to have a new deed to the Zhou placers, and he was throwing the Chinese off his claim.

Arnest immediately recognized the white man—his name was George Winchester and he had visited the Zhou placers frequently. He was always trying to get them to sell their placers. He was from Hangtown.

Arnest was the only Simmons who had approached the Zhou family; the other Cherokees had remained outside the fire circle in the dark, with their weapons cocked. Arnest didn't know what to do, but his first thoughts were to get the Sheriff to come here and disarm everyone before this became a massive slaughter. His prayers were answered shortly when both Sheriff Rogers and Sergeant Beavers walked up to the fire and demanded to know what was going on.

Winchester showed the Sheriff his pieces of paper that deeded the Zhou placers to a mining company in Hangtown. He claimed that Chin had sold the placers to the mining company several days ago and was now refusing to leave the property.

The Sheriff told Winchester that there was nothing in the California law that allowed an angry new owner of a piece of property to attack the former owner in the middle of the night and drive the old owners off the premises. Only he, the Sheriff, could do that—and he wasn't about to do anything like that this evening. The County Judge made those kinds of decisions. The Sheriff took Winchester's deeds and carefully placed them in his uniform pocket. Then he told Winchester that he and all his men must leave the premises immediately; Winchester would be contacted by the County Court about a hearing on this case.

Sergeant Beavers ordered Winchester's men to release the Zhou family and return their weapons. Then the Sheriff told Sergeant Beavers to set up a perimeter to protect this property for the next several days until the Judge could make some sense out of this 'claim jump'.

In the days that followed, the Zhou family began collecting up their equipment and packing some of it; perhaps they were planning to leave the gold field rather than fight. When Arnest spoke privately with Chin, the leader of the Zhou family repeated over and over that they did not want any more bloodshed—they had already lost one son to gunfighting and hate and the family was not willing to lose the remaining members of the family. Since the Zhou family was terribly exposed as they slept in their tents at their placers, Arnest arranged for the four members of the family to bunk in the Simmons cabin. It was crowded, but it was safe.

Chin had his boys, Ho and Kim, pull their long-toms out of the muck at the bottom of the riverbed and stack them on the riverbank. Then, at Howey's suggestion, the troughs were moved to a point behind the Simmons' corral. Everyone knew that the rainy season was close, so everything that the Zhou family was doing made a lot of sense.

Chin had said very little about all that had happened recently, but one evening he decided to talk with Arnest and Jean, and ask for more advice. He began the discussion with, "The last time we had one of these talks about what to do with our children, I told you that I wanted to send Yang back to the Nebraska Territory. Well, I didn't do it, and now he is dead."

Jean answered quickly with "But his death is not your fault, Chin. There was no way you were going to get him to return to Nebraska—he was too old to force him to doing anything he didn't want to do."

Chin nodded in agreement. "We Sa sent a letter to my wife, Mi Yan, telling her about Yang's death. I suspect we will hear from Mi Yan in about three months, begging us to return home before there is more bloodshed."

After a pause, he continued with, "None of the four of us here has any desire to mine for gold any more. I think I can tell you this, Arnest, in confidence, but we have panned more gold than we ever thought we would. Of course, we were one of the first families to come here because my former employer in St. Louis, Hi Te, sent us a letter almost six months before the government made the announcement about the gold in California. He told us about the gold rumors then, and we were able to move here and pan for gold when the nuggets were big. There aren't any big nuggets left in this river now."

"There is time to return East before the winter snows come," Arnest suggested. "If you go back through the Humboldt River and Salt Lake City the heat will not be so unbearable at this time of year."

Chin agreed. Then he asked Arnest and Jean, "When do you all plan to return East?"

Arnest looked at Jean and Jean looked at Arnest. "We aren't collecting as much gold as we had hoped this year," Arnest replied, "but we don't want to stay if this settlement becomes a place where people feud with one another and kill and maim to get more gold."

"Would you consider leaving now?" Chin asked the two Simmons.

"That is a very hard question to answer," Arnest replied. "We must guard against becoming greedy—knowing that our family is making five or six times as much money as we would if we were back home. But the Cherokee Nation Territory is a safe place to live in, and I'm not sure that Coloma really is safe right now."

Then Arnest added, "Tim and Bixby have a lot to say about whether or not we go home now, also."

"Why do you ask us this question?" Jean asked.

"Because it had occurred to me that if you want to flee from California now, we could all go together before the snows come. The Truckee Pass and Carson Pass will close soon for the winter," Chin answered.

"I will certainly ask Tim and Bixby and our boys how they feel about going home now," Arnest replied. "They may surprise us—they may be ready to go home."

Jean made no statement, but she knew that her boys had greatly differing views from their father about where 'home' was. Both Renwe and Staufo loved their jobs, and Staufo was spending more time at the Chin tents than he was at the Simmons cabin. He probably wouldn't be willing to leave without We Sa. Then the more Jean thought about it, the more it became clear that Chin was fully expecting his only daughter, We Sa to go with him back to New Fort Kearney. If she returned to Kearney then Staufo would probably tag along with them.

Two days later Sergeant Beavers visited the Zhou family and told them that were expected to appear in the Eldorado County Courthouse in Coloma the following Monday to present their case before Judge Albrecht, the county Presiding Judge. "The courthouse is the same building as the county office," Beavers told them, "only the county office is on the ground floor and the court uses the top floor."

"Do not fail to appear," Beavers warned Chin. "Cause, if you do, the judge will give your claim to Winchester in a second." Chin thanked the Deputy for the information, and assured him that he and his family would be there.

That evening, right after the evening meal, the Zhous announced that they were going to visit a Chinese family a couple miles away, so they mounted their horses and started north. The cabin was suddenly very quiet, so Jean decided to call for a family council while the Zhous were gone.

She made-up a brew of apple juice with cinnamon and bitters, and heated it so it gave off the aroma of the cinnamon. After she gave everyone a mugful, she sat down next to Arnest and declared the meeting in session.

"The reason we are all here tonight," Arnest began, "is to discuss what we plan to do in the future. Before we ever came to California we all sat beside the South Platte River and agreed that it was best to travel west and seek our fortune in California. Well, here we are two years later. We have plenty of gold for all, and we are all healthy and safe in our cabin. But the gold-sluicing season comes to an end in the next month, and many of us will be out of work. So I put this question to each of you: What do you want to do now, and in the next year?"

No one wanted to be first, but Howey finally raised his hand and agreed to speak. "I been thinking a lot about this whole California business ever since Claire died," he began. "At first I kept telling myself that this was gawd-awful country that man should never have attempted to tame."

After he cleared his throat he continued, "And then I realized that I don't really hate California. The thing I hate is the way we got here. Who in their right mind would live between Salt Lake City and the Sierra Nevada Mountains? But Coloma isn't all that bad. The gold miners around us are just people like ourselves, and they come from all over this country, and maybe from all over this world. A few are bad apples, but not many of them."

"Why should I go back home?" he asked the group. "Because it's a lot greener there than it is here? I don't care about the 'green' around me. I'm willing to irrigate to raise food for myself and work for someone else to make a living. And I can 'blend' in around here pretty easy—there's lots of Mexicans and other Indians around here who look a lot like me.

"I certainly wouldn't stay in California because the land is so fertile. Hell, there's not a place east of the Mississippi River that has soil as bad as California. When did I convince myself that I am a farmer anyway?"

Then Howey realized that he had not answered the question that he was asked. "So here's what I'm going to do," he answered. "As soon as we're through sluicing for gold I'm gonna get myself a job with the Sheriff's Office and learn how to be a Peace Officer. If that's not enough to keep me busy then I'm going to buy some land close to Coloma and raise grapes. There are half a dozen wineries in this county, and they can't get anyone to grow grapes for them!"

With this announcement, Howey sat down.

Arnest and Jean were pleased that Howey spoke so forcefully. Maybe Renwe and Staufo would do the same.

Bixby was the next to raise his hand. "Howey and I have talked about this a lot, and we are both agreed that the best place to get old is where the weather is warm a good part of the year and you don't have to worry about the people who live around you comin' in some night and sendin' you on to the next world with a Colt Forty-Five."

Everyone agreed. Bixby continued: "So I have no plans to become a Peace Officer 'cause I know the Sheriff wouldn't hire me anyway. But if I buy land close to Howey's place I can get him to grow his grapes on my land too, and I can go up into the Sierra Nevada and trap for beaver just like I have all the rest of my life."

As he sat down he closed with, "So I guess you would say that I'm not goin' anywhere when we decide to stop playin' the gold miner game."

There was a pause, and Bixby added, "I hope the rest of you remember the way home to the South Platte River. I don't think there's any other way home except through that hell-hole called the Humboldt River."

Was anyone going to return to Fort Lupton?

There were no more volunteers, so Arnest asked Tim to speak next.

"I was hopin' to be last," he mentioned, "because I'm not real sure what to say. But I will tell you that the Sheriff has promised that the county will sell me the forge, and the land beneath it. You all know that I don't want to be a farmer, but I like to be around farm people. In another ten years there won't be a gold miner left in this county—the gold will play-out just like it always does. Then I can do the blacksmithing job in peace and quiet."

Renwe and Staufo were quiet in the back of the cabin. They obviously didn't want to say anything. But Jean coaxed them closer to the fireplace and asked them to speak. Renwe was first: "We came here a couple of years ago to mine for gold, and I have yet to 'sluice' the first day of my life. I have the best job a person could have at the saw mill, and with the kind of money that I'll get when we split up the gold, I'll be able to set up my own saw mill somewhere in this county or maybe on the other side of Sacramento. So I don't plan to go back to Fort Lupton either."

That left only Staufo, and he was struggling about what to say. "I don't know how much I want to tell you people," he began, 'because I really haven't decided whether California or the Kansas Territory or the Cherokee Nation Territory is the place to live."

"But one thing I can tell you," Staufo continued, "is that I'm not goin' any-where unless We Sa goes with me. That woman means too much to me to ever let her go."

Then he added, "I'm sorry, Arnest and Jean, if you expected me to marry some fine Cherokee girl back home so we could continue the Simmons name there, but it's not working out that way. We may decide to go to Fort Lupton or to the New Fort Kearney, or to Monterrey. And the reason I mention Monterrey is because the man who owns the wagon-works where I work is planning to set up a larger plant somewhere close to Monterrey, and he is goin' to sell a bunch of those wagons to California people for a long time. The day will come when everybody in California knows about Studebaker wagons."

Jean and Arnest kept it short: "We're going back to the South Platte River and grow cattle feed, and love it," they said. "Then we're going to try to convince Eileen and Marcy and their families to come to the South Platte River also."

The session was over.

Right after the meeting, the first thing that Jean and Arnest told Staufo was something that they had felt in their hearts for many months: "We would be proud to have We Sa as our daughter-in-law" they told him. "You would be a fool to ever let that woman get away." Staufo broke into a wide grin. "I been worried about what you were going to say," he told them. "Thanks for telling me now."

When the Zhous returned from their visit, Chin told Arnest that he may have a buyer for his claim. Then he added, "But I have to get the court to throw out those fake deeds that Winchester has shown to the Sheriff before I can do any selling."

That night, since the Simmons cabin was so crowded, the boys decided to sleep outside for the remainder of the night. The weather was cool when the sun went down, and there was a light breeze from the west. The breeze kept the mosquitoes away.

Early the next morning, about an hour before sunrise, the boys saw a fire blazing at the Zhou claim. The main tent with the red, white, and blue flag was on fire. They hollered 'fire' at the top of their lungs several times, and took off for the claim. The people inside the Simmons cabin heard the 'fire' alarm and they immediately began putting on their boots to see what was going on. About two minutes after the boys ran toward the Zhou claim, two shots rang out, coming from that direction.

As Arnest reached the Zhou campsite he saw that only the one tent was burning. He also noticed people running away from the fire. Then, suddenly, it became very quiet.

Bixby, who had arrived on the scene late, was the first to find a body lying in the shrubbery about 100 feet from the campfire site. When he rolled him over he realized that it was George Winchester.

Arnest knew that he better get the Sheriff involved in a hurry, so he ran back to the cabin, took both percussion rifles from their places in the kitchen, and stepped outside. In quick succession he fired two shots into the air, and everyone close by was immediately awakened. He put the rifles back in the cabin, and then tripped over some sidearms just outside the cabin door. There was very little light, but he saw the two pepperboxes that belonged to Renwe and Staufo, and the two derringers that belonged to Ho and Kim Zhou. He breathed a sign of relief—who ever fired their weapons at the Zhou campsite were strangers—the four boys were unarmed.

As expected, Sergeant Beavers arrived in a few minutes. He immediately took charge of the investigation. The tent that had been on fire was now reduced to rubble. He told the boys to get the campfire going again so they could see what was going on. In a few minutes two other Deputies arrived at the scene.

Bixby immediately showed Beavers the dead man, and no one got close to the dead body at the edge of the clearing. Beavers told one of the Deputies to return to the bivouac and bring every Deputy back to this site since they were going to have to guard the site until daybreak. Then they could figure out what had happened.

The boys built-up the fire in the center of the campground so they could have more light. Sergeant Beavers examined Winchester's body. He had two shots high on the center of his back, and in his greatcoat he had two leather pokes that contained small amounts of gold. He was armed with a Colt revolver.

The tents that remained had all been ransacked, and someone had cut deep furrows in the ground inside the tents with a piece of sharp steel or a knife. They were looking for leather gold pokes.

After daybreak the Sheriff and the County Coroner showed up to investigate the murder. They determined that whoever had overrun this campsite had searched frantically for gold. The Sheriff surmised that "One thief shot the other." The gold in the two pokes found on Winchester's body held less than twenty dollars apiece. The Coroner took the body to a makeshift morgue behind the forge.

About noon that day Arnest noticed that the Sheriff was talking to a man intently at the edge of the river. When they were finished, the Sheriff approached Arnest and told him that he wanted to speak to the two Chinese boys who were involved in the fire last night. Arnest took the Sheriff to the Simmons cabin but the boys were not there. Jean said they had probably gone hunting because they were so bored. Renwe and Staufo had already left for their jobs that morning.

The two flintlock rifles in the kitchen were missing, which probably meant that that Ho and Kim had gone hunting. When evening came the Sheriff left two Deputies on the site, and gave them instructions to notify him as soon as the Chinese boys returned home.

Right after sundown Ho and Kim returned to the Simmons cabin with a fox and a prairie chicken. They were starting to clean the rifles and dress the animals when one of the Deputies who was guarding the Zhou claim approached the boys. As soon as he recognized them, he called for the other Deputy to come quick.

Once the two Deputies were there, they pointed their sidearms at the two boys, forced them to the ground, and tied them with rope. They told Arnest that they were taking the two men to the new jail. Try as he may, Arnest could not convince the Deputies that Ho and Kim had nothing to do with the murder last night.

Chin returned to the Simmons cabin about an hour later, and the Simmons family told him that his boys had been taken to jail. Chin immediately wanted to know what was going on, so he stormed over to the jail. The Deputies told him that there was a man who was ready to testify that the Zhou boys had shot the guy named Winchester in the back. So their instructions were to keep his boys in the jail until the investigation was complete.

The next day the Sheriff came to the Simmons cabin and told Chin that he would have to keep the Zhou brothers in the jail for the present time, but no harm would come to them. For one thing, the man who claimed to have seen the murder the night before lived a long way from the Zhou claim and he would have to explain his presence there at the time the murder occurred. Also, there was no light in the area when the murder occurred. He would have a hard time convincing anyone that he witnessed the Zhou boys shooting Winchester.

Meanwhile, the Sheriff was hoping that someone else in the neighborhood had seen something that night that would shed light on what really happened. "We will never know what Winchester's motive was for raiding the Zhou placers early that morning, but it looks like it was pure robbery," the Sheriff concluded.

On the following Monday, Chin and We Sa Zhou appeared before the Eldorado County Presiding Judge, as they had been directed. The company who claimed to own the 'deeds' that Winchester was forced to give to the Sheriff a week earlier were present also. Arnest and Jean were there, and had indicated that they could testify about what happened the night the Winchester raiding party took the Zhou's as prisoners.

The presiding judge made it clear that this was a hearing about American Mining's claim to the Zhou placers—the murder that had occurred three days earlier would be discussed in court at a later hearing.

The Judge indicated that the first witness he had intended to call was Mr. Winchester, an employee of the American Mining Company, but since Mr. Winchester was now dead, the court would proceed without his testimony. Immediately a man sitting next to the owner of American Mining jumped up and began screaming about the Zhou brothers—"and the reason, your Honor, that Mr. Winchester can't be here today is because those Chinese brothers shot him in the back last week! They are cold-blooded murderers!"

The Judge asked the man to sit down, and then he called for the Sheriff. "Take that man," the judge told the Sheriff, "the one with the big mouth, and put him in the county jail for now. I will deal with him when this hearing is over."

The man with the big mouth stood up to say something else, but the owner of American Mining grabbed him by his pants pockets and pulled him back down onto the bench. Then the Sheriff took the man out of the court chambers and everyone sat in silence.

The judge called Arnest to the witness stand, but the owner of the company that Winchester worked for, American Mining, Inc., protested, saying that Arnest Simmons was an Indian and a California court could hear no testimony from an Indian, or a Mexican, or a Chinese, or anyone who wasn't an American citizen white person.

"Your Honor," the owner of American Mining said, "we know that you are well aware of the laws passed by the Legislature of the State of California one year ago concerning who is and who is not a reliable witness in a California court of law. Mr. Simmons does not qualify as a reliable witness."

There was a pause in the discussion, so Arnest stood up told the group, "Your honor, I am a citizen of the United States of America. I became a citizen twenty years ago, in North Carolina!"

"But you're an Indian", the American Mining company owner blurted out, "and you cannot testify in this court!"

The judge told everyone to settle down, and he elected to call the county 'keeper-of-records' to the witness stand instead. The keeper-of-records deferred to a man who had come from Monterrey, a specialist at the State Records office, to testify concerning the validity of the deeds given to the Sheriff by Winchester.

Everyone was agreed that this was an acceptable procedure. After the man from the state was sworn in, the judge asked him about the Winchester deeds.

The witness pulled no punches: "These deeds are obvious fakes," the man told the judge. "They fail in many ways. For example, they are printed on the wrong kind of paper and they have two mis-spelled words in them. The real, official deeds have no mis-spelled words in them."

The owner of American Mining was attempting to object to something, but the judge dropped the gavel on the hard wooden block, and called for silence. "This claim by the American Mining Company is disavowed by this court, and I would warn the owner of American Mining that he may be called into this court to answer for his actions in this matter at a later date. If he falsified land deeds then he must answer for that. For the time being, this court is adjourned."

This might have been a time for great celebration by the Zhou and Simmons families, but the truth was, Ho and Kim were in jail only a short distance from the city hall, both charged with the murder of a hoodlum named Winchester. After the Chins and the Simmons and Tim and Bixby left the court they went by the jail to see how Ho and Kim were doing. The boys said they were all right, but the food was terrible. "Can We Sa bring some real food over here in the evenings?" Ho asked.

We Sa agreed to do so, starting today. Then Ho asked the obvious question, "How long are we going to have to stay in this jail?"

No one knew the answer to that question. So Chin asked his boys to 'take it easy for a few days, and we'll have some answers for you in a week or so.' Chin noticed that there was no wood for the fireplace, so he told Ho and Kim that he would bring a little firewood and some extra blankets so they could stay warm at night. The nights were getting a little chilly.

The man that the judge had sent to jail earlier was sitting in the first cell. Arnest approached him and asked him what his name was. The man just looked at Arnest and remained silent. Then he uttered some unintelligible words about "Them Chinks are gonna pay for killin' my brother-in-law."

As the group was walking back to the cabin they tried to figure out who the 'man with the big mouth' was in the court—the one that was going to spend this night in the jail unless he and the Judge could settle their differences. Bixby broke off from the group and told them that he was going to Sally Jo's saloon to find out who the man was.

About an hour later Bixby showed up with a tall man who was carrying a briefcase. The tall man's name was Thadeus Fit. He was offered some food at the dinner table, and he ate it. When the eating time was over, Bixby explained that his guest was the only person in Coloma who knew anything about murder trials—he was employed by Sally Jo Timmons and his job was to keep the saloon 'within the laws of the State of California and Eldorado County'. Mr. Fit contradicted Bixby's introduction though: he had never participated in a murder trial before.

"When we walked past the jail, the Sheriff was taking the 'man with the big mouth' to the courthouse, so he will probably be released by the judge pretty soon," Bixby announced.

"Mrs. Timmons told me the day after the Zhou brothers were put in jail to collect all the information on this case," Mr. Fit explained. "She is afraid that the facts in the case will be mishandled and reshaped to assure a guilty verdict when the case comes to the county court. She doesn't want that to happen."

The group spent the next two hours looking over the supposed 'evidence' that would be offered by the county, to include an on-the-scene witness who would testify that he saw the two Zhou brothers shoot Winchester in the back, plus a county coroner's report that would say it was impossible to determine the caliber of the bullets that killed Winchester. At the end of the session Renwe remembered that the reason Bixby had gone over to Sally Jo's saloon was to find out who the 'man with the big mouth' was.

"Who is Mr. Big Mouth?" Renwe asked Bixby.

"It turns out," Bixby responded, that he is George Winchester's brother-in-law. His name is Howard Bolender. He works for the American Mining Company. But the most important thing about Howard Bolender is that he is constantly at odds with Sheriff Rogers about crime-control in Eldorado County. He thinks of himself as the 'protector of the people', and favors vigilante action over county court action. He lives in Hangtown and supposedly has participated in three lynchings in that part of the county in the past three years. He is trying to do the same thing in Hangtown as they are doing in San Francisco right now—vigilante action against accused prisoners."

"So this man is capable of taking the law into his own hands," Arnest stated.

"Absolutely," Mr. Fit responded.

After Mr. Fit left, Chin announced that the family's placers were being sold to the Chinese family they had visited a few days earlier. "We're tired of being the target of someone's anger in this settlement," Chin told the group.

"What is the new owner going to do with your claim, Chin?" Howey asked.

Chin had a quick answer: "They are going to sell it to someone next spring. If no one buys it they will sell it to the hydraulic miners."

🍁   🍁   🍁

An hour later, Herman, Sally Jo Timmons' driver, rode up to the cabin door on a horse and asked to speak with Arnest and Chin. The three men met outside.

"Mrs. Timmons told me to tell you that she has to talk with the three of you—Arnest and Jean Simmons and Chin Zhou, sometime tonight. This is very important. You must come—all three of you. Mrs. Timmons doesn't want to be seen near your cabin in the next couple of days, so she cannot come here."

Arnest went into the cabin and brought Jean outside. "Sally Jo wants to talk to the three of us tonight," Arnest told Jean. "Are you agreed to meeting her?"

Jean nodded in the affirmative.

Herman gave them more instructions. "When Yang was buried near the river, you will remember a small house that is painted yellow near the gravesite, only 50 yards to the west. It is the only yellow house in town. Come there as soon as the moon appears in the western sky, which will be about two hours from now." Herman turned to Arnest and Jean and added, "Please do not tell your boys where you are going—we cannot afford to have 'loose' talk in the settlement."

Everyone nodded in the affirmative, and Herman mounted his horse and left.

"One thing that is for sure," Jean said before they returned to the cabin. "This has everything to do with Ho and Kim."

❦   ❦   ❦

Two hours later the trio was walking up a narrow set of stone steps that led to the yellow house. When they reached the front door, Sally Jo appeared at the front door and she ushered them inside.

"Thank you for coming," she said. "I am concerned about what is happening in this village right now and I fear for the lives of your boys, Chin. Some people want to offer them as a sacrifice for a brainless murder that occurred on your claim last week. I aim to stop that sacrifice right here and now."

When they sat down around a table, Sally Jo lit a kerosene lantern and the trio realized that there was a fifth person in the room. It was Sergeant Beavers. He took off his hat and sat down at the table.

Sally Jo began the conversation with, "There are some things you ought to know about Billy Beavers and myself, so I'll get that out of the way right now."

"First, I have told everyone that my husband was killed in South Dakota, but I have never filled in the details. He was a Lakota Sioux, the smartest man in the Trenton Mines, and he was in charge of two hundred miners who respected him. But some of them, when they found out he was a full-blooded Sioux Indian, learned to hate his guts. One of them shot him down in cold-blood one night in front of our saloon, and a jury of twelve drunken miners set the killer free because it was a case of 'self-defense'. The problem was, my husband was unarmed at the time. Matter of fact, he never carried a firearm."

"So you know what I think about murder trials and juries made up of miners," she said.

She continued with, "The only person who tried to stand up for my rights was a young Corporal in the Cavalry who tried to point out the vast inconsistencies in the trial of my husband's murderer. He made it so uncomfortable for the state and county police that the Army decided to transfer him to St. Louis."

Sergeant Beavers took up the story: "Right after the Mexican War ended, while I was in St. Louis, I got a letter from Sally Jo telling me that she was moving to either San Francisco or Sacramento to get away from the poisoned politics of South Dakota, and she mentioned that if I ever needed a job I could count on her to find me one."

"To make a long story short," he continued, "I showed up on her doorstep in Coloma several years later and she immediately got me a job as a Deputy Sheriff."

Turning her attention to Chin, Arnest, and Jean, Sally Jo said, "Did Thadeus Fit help you all understand what is going on here?"

"Yes, he was very helpful," Jean answered. "But none of us knows what to do now," she added.

"The reason no one sought justice for my husband in South Dakota was because he was an Indian," Sally Jo said. "The reason that no one will seek justice for Ho and Kim Zhou here in Coloma is because they are Chinese."

Beavers spoke: "The county coroner is about as incompetent as they come—the people around him have him convinced that the caliber of the bullets that killed Winchester cannot be determined because they are too mangled. But the truth is, the bullets that killed Winchester came from a modern Colt revolver, and there's nobody in California that has that kind of weapon except Peace Officers. Winchester was shot by someone working for the Law."

"Which explains why some people never want this case to come to the courthouse." Beavers continued. "Telling the truth in this murder causes problems for too many well-heeled people in the county. One of those people is Howard Bolender, Winchester's brother-in-law. Bolender wants to hang anyone who gets in his way collecting gold—he has seen the glint of gold and he wants lots of it."

Chin Zhou had said nothing so far. He opened up with, "If what you say is true, then my boys will be hanged for Winchester's murder, no matter how many inconsistencies there are in the evidence presented at their trial."

"True, true," Beavers responded.

"What is the Sheriff's part in all this?" Arnest asked.

"He has no part in this murder," Sally Jo explained. "He is one of those people who seek 'justice for all' but there are snakes in the grass everywhere you look. That's what gold does to people. If we were in New Orleans, we would say that the Sheriff is a 'lily white.'"

Beavers added, "That's one reason why Sheriff Rogers is not here tonight. He must be told nothing because he will be forced to speak to the public if the Zhou brothers do not come to trial. If we get Ho and Kim out of jail, he will catch 'hell' from some people here who want someone else to be the Sheriff."

Chin wanted to slow this discussion down a bit. He turned to Arnest and Jean and asked an obvious question: "Why should you Cherokees become involved in the trial of two Chinese men that you didn't even know two years ago? What if this plot backfires and you find yourselves surrounded by people like Bolender? Is there a chance that one of you might be hanged by vigilantes?"

Arnest had an immediate answer: "Remember a couple of weeks ago when you asked if we wanted to 'flee' with you back to the East, and leave this place where there is so much gunfighting and killing? You started us thinking about that prospect, and Jean and I are ready to leave. We asked everyone in our family what they wanted to do, and every one of them wants to leave Coloma but stay in California. They want to move some distance away from all this turmoil, and perhaps return later when the gold fever dies out."

It was Sally Jo's time to speak: "There is only one person at this table tonight who can approve what we are talking about, and that person is you, Chin Zhou. Do you want your boys to take their chances at an Eldorado County murder trial, or do you want to get them out of jail and send them home to the Nebraska Territory?"

Chin answered immediately: "I want to take them back to Nebraska, now."

Sally Jo reminded the group that "Everyone in the settlement assumes that the Zhou family came from San Francisco, and we need to keep everyone thinking that way. When we get the boys out of jail they will go east and the big posse will head west."

Beavers handed Chin a small, highly polished key. "Give this key to Tim," he instructed. "Tim will immediately recognize it as the master key that the lock manufacturer in Connecticut sent to us mistakenly with our order last spring. No one knows about this key but myself, Tim, and now all of you. Once you get Ho and Kim out of the jail you lock everything back up and let some investigating team figure out how this jailbreak happened."

"What do we do with the master key then?" Arnest asked.

"You place it at the foot of the fence post in the northeast corner of your corral, Arnest," Sally Jo replied, "and Herman will pick it up the next day to return it to Sergeant Beavers."

Everyone was tired, but nothing had been said so far about the details of getting Ho and Kim out of jail. Beavers and Sally Jo had all the details.

"The breakout must occur around midnight two nights from now, for two important reasons," Sally Jo explained. "Number one is that there will be no moon whatsoever that night. Number two is that my saloon is sponsoring a long evening of free drinking and entertainment in the big empty lot behind the saloon, and it will begin about ten o'clock. I have arranged for the biggest fight in the history of Coloma to break-out close to midnight, and Sergeant Beavers will receive a plea from Herman or myself to come and restore peace to the celebration."

Beavers continued the story: "As soon as the plea for help comes, I grab up every Deputy around and we go behind the saloon to restore peace. The jail guard that night will be Deputy Klink, and he is our all-time, never-ending alcoholic problem. There will be an open bottle of whiskey close to the jail guard's desk, and he will drink himself under the table in twenty minutes. You people are responsible for getting Ho and Kim out of that jail and on their way to Nebraska, and I don't want to know anything about the details."

"How do we make sure that Sheriff Rogers doesn't become involved in this jailbreak?" Chin asked. "What if he decides to visit the jail at the very worst of times?"

There was silence for a moment, and then Sally Jo volunteered her services. "I am inviting both the Sheriff and his wife to be my special guests at this party—we are celebrating five years of good times in Coloma, and I will make sure that they don't leave the premises. That may be hard to do, but I'll keep them there well past midnight."

Then Beavers added, "If any of your family remains in the Coloma area, make sure that they stay out of town for at least a week or two, to let all the furor die down. And please, please, don't shoot anybody. My Deputies are all good people, even Klink, and I don't want them to get hurt."

There were no further questions, so the group went their separate ways.

CHAPTER 14

Breaking Camp

The next morning, before Renwe and Staufo left for work, Arnest got everyone together and told them that Ho and Kim would be busted out of jail two nights from now. Sally Jo Timmons was going to give a big party behind her saloon to celebrate her five years in Coloma, and during that celebration the boys would be released. "I am glad that there are no little children in this household," he said, "because little people don't know how to keep secrets. All of you do know how to keep secrets, and you don't tell anybody anything."

He continued with, "Tonight we will go over the specifics of the jail break. Tim, we have the master key to get into the jail through the rear door. Sergeant Beavers insists that every one of us clear out of this settlement for at least the next two weeks because there are vigilante groups that may want to make someone in this cabin pay with their lives after the jail break becomes widely known. We will all meet here after the evening meal tonight to discuss the specifics of the event. Then the following night we get Ho and Kim out of jail."

He ended the session with, "Everybody go back to work, and do whatever has to be done to get your body safely out of this settlement tomorrow night."

Shortly after the morning session, Bixby announced that he was going to the Parker farm. "We don't need any more chickens," he was told. "I'm not buying chickens today," he responded. "I'm lookin' for a place to sleep for the next two weeks."

He took his favorite mule and headed for the Parker farm.

We Sa was taking food to her brothers at the jail twice a day now. Chin told her not to say anything to them about the jail break today because it may cause confusion in their minds. "You tell them about the jail break when you take them the second meal tomorrow, and tell them to be fully dressed and ready to ride by midnight." Chin told her. We Sa understood.

Tim, Jean, Chin, and Arnest suddenly had a lot of time on their hands. About the only thing they could accomplish today was to buy food for those who were traveling east—five people in all. Chin insisted that there would be six people, four in his family and two in the Simmons family, so Jean packed for six. Jean knew that Staufo would go in whichever direction We Sa went, which meant that there may be five people going to Salt Lake City, and there again there may be seven. Everyone else was pretty well accounted for.

While Arnest was at the general store buying food and fresh ammunition, Jean wrote a letter to her girls at home, saying that the family was finally coming back East. She would write again when they reached the Kansas Territory and the South Platte River. Then she wrote a short letter to the O'Leary family in San Francisco telling them that the Simmons had to flee for their lives after a murder was committed in the settlement, and the O'Leary gold for the last month was buried at the southeast corner fencepost in the Simmons corral. The O'Learys could have the cabin and the corral if they wanted it. The Simmons family did not have the time to sell their claim at the river.

Howey methodically checked the leather traces, saddles, and bridles for the animals, both the horses and the mules. Tim checked the general condition of the animals, and it was decided that all of them were in good enough health to make the trip either west or east. Chin had come to California with a total of six horses (five to transport people and one pack horse). Arnest knew that there would be only five people headed east—Arnest, Jean, Chin, Ho, and Kim. So they needed ten horses—six from the Chins and four from the Simmons. It all worked out pretty well.

❧   ❧   ❧

At sunset Bixby returned from the Parker farm and told the group that all the arrangements had been made to keep himself, Tim, Renwe, Staufo, and We Sa at the farm for the time being. Chin was present when Bixby returned, so there was no discussion about which way We Sa was headed the next night.

As they settled in for the night, Arnest met with Staufo outside the cabin and reminded him that it was We Sa's task (and Staufo's task) to tell Chin what they planned to do the next evening. "By early tomorrow morning I want him to know what you two are planning to do. You aren't going to spring this decision on him at the last moment, you hear," Arnest asserted.

Staufo nodded and said he would take care of it.

Jean made a trip to the Lone Star of Texas saloon, to deliver her beautiful dress and all its accessories back to Sally Jo. She had arranged with Herman to have them placed back in Sally Jo's wardrobe closet on the top floor of the saloon. As time had passed, the true identity of the dress became known: It was Sally Jo's dress from the very beginning.

The last order of business was the division of the gold to the Simmons, Tim Wisnant, and Elias Bixby. They had not made as much money the second year (as they did the first), but the two-year total was $22,000.00 or $3,143.00 apiece. Sally Jo Timmons was a big collector of Philadelphia gold coins, so she had given them twenty-dollar and five-dollar gold pieces in exchange for all their nuggets and gold dust. She knew that the gold pieces were a lot more spendable than raw gold. She made the same deal with Chin.

❧   ❧   ❧

The next morning, bright and early, Renwe and Staufo saddled up their horses to go to work. At the end of the work day they would go to the Parker farm. We Sa and Staufo approached Chin and asked that they take a short walk toward the big trees behind the corral. Chin was confused, but he agreed to walk with them.

When they were behind the corral, Staufo began the conversation with, "Mr. Zhou, We Sa and I have been talking about getting married for a lot of months now, and we're at the point now where we have to settle some things. I want to marry your daughter, Sir, and take her with me to Sacramento."

Chin made no reply at first. "Sacramento," he repeated. "Why have your waited this late to tell me these things?" Chin asked the two.

"Because, Poppy," We Sa explained, "we were afraid of what you might say."

"No, no," Chin replied. "That is not what you mean. What you are really saying is that your decision to marry has already been made and it doesn't matter what I say now. I have no vote in this decision."

"Yes sir," Staufo returned, "that's about the way it is. We are going to Sacramento and we are going to get married there. What we want is your blessing on this union, because we both respect you so much."

There was a quiet time. Then Chin responded with, "I guess that young people do today whatever they want to do. I knew this was coming, but I wasn't sure what to say when it happened. Yes, the two of you have my blessing. I will tell Ho and Kim about your plans to live in Sacramento when I see them tonight."

"Poppy," We Sa said, "shall I take the gold that I sewed into my bodice and return it to you?"

Chin laughed. "No, no," he told his daughter, "that is your money. You deserve it. Easy come, easy go!"

Then he added, "We Sa, do you want to take the food to your brothers this evening, or do you want to leave earlier with Staufo?"

"I want to take food to them tonight," We Sa responded, "and I will tell them to be ready to leave Coloma tonight. But I will not tell them that Staufo and I are going the other way—to the west. You must tell them that later."

The old man nodded in agreement and the three of them returned to the cabin.

Arnest and Jean were waiting in front of the cabin. They were examining Chin's facial expression closely to determine if everything had gone all right in the woods. When Chin saw them he smiled, and they knew that the plan for Staufo and We Sa was set.

"I will leave work at the wagon-works at the usual time," Staufo told everyone. "At the end of the work day I will come here and We Sa and I will go to the Parker farm." He kissed We Sa, mounted his horse, and started down the lane toward his work. Then he stopped, turned around, and returned to the front of the cabin.

"I think I forgot about something," he said. "When I return this evening I may not see some of you. He hugged Chin Zhou, then his mother, then his father. There were tears in his eyes. Then he reminded Tim, Bixby, and Renwe that he would see all of them at the Parker farm late this evening.

He returned to his mother, and she was in tears. "A mother always gets to cry when one of her sons decides to marry, and this is no exception to the rule," she said. "I wish the best for both of you, and someday, when you expect it the least, Arnest and I will show up at your front door. You just wait and see!"

Staufo hugged his mother again, and was gone in an instant.

Not all of the decisions for this evening had already been made.

Bixby stated that he and Howey were going to remain at the cabin until everyone else had cleared the settlement. "We only have fifteen miles to travel tonight, and there's no reason to be in a hurry about it," he said.

Howey agreed. Tim's only comment was "I'm travelin' with those two tonight (Bixby and Howey). It's my job to make sure the master key ends up at the foot of the fence post in the northeast corner of the corral.

Then he added, "I better not bury that key too deep because it looks like the rain is comin' in from the west, and that corral may be under water by midnight tonight."

"What a night for the monsoon season to start," Howey commented. Then he asked Arnest how far they planned to ride tonight.

"We won't push the horses real hard," Arnest responded. "We will ride all night, then rest about halfway between here and the Truckee Pass. I won't really feel safe until we reach the Truckee Meadows," he added.

Everyone standing there in front of the cabin knew that they had glossed-over the most important issue this evening—getting Ho and Kim out of the jail and not rousing a big posse that would be nipping at their heels all the time they were fleeing for Truckee Pass.

Bixby reminded Chin, Arnest, and Jean that "You will not know if the posse has taken the bait and headed for Sacramento. This county has some good trackers, and they might figure out that you headed East."

We Sa took the evening meal to Ho and Kim wearing a poncho, and it was a good thing that she did. The monsoon rains began just a few minutes later. She entered the jail, approached Deputy Klink, and gave him a sweet roll, something she had been doing for the jail guard for the past three days. While he was munching on the sweet roll, We Sa slipped a tray through the pass-through to her brothers. As Ho took the tray she looked him straight in the eyes and said, "Be prepared to travel tonight. Be fully clothed by midnight. The men will come through the back door, where the outhouse is located."

Ho understood.

That said, she left. She returned to the cabin in the rain, and found Staufo waiting for her. She could feel tears coming down her cheeks. She hugged her man as they stepped inside the cabin. This was a big rain, and the water was beginning to leak at spots in the roof. All day long she had been nervous about the small part she played in this jailbreak. But she knew that she had said the right words to her older brother, and he had nodded in response. So far, so good!

Both We Sa and Staufo were questioning their original decision to leave for the Parker farm immediately. "What if something goes wrong?" she asked Tim and

Bixby. "What if you need every gun this family can come up with to get Ho and Kim out of the jail?"

Tim licked his lower lip and replied with, "This jail break is going to go one of two ways. Either I unlock the back door, open it up, unlock the cell door, and Ho and Kim and I are out of there in less than a minute. Or, something goes wrong and Ho and Kim never make it to the Truckee Pass. I'm not willing to shoot anyone to make this plan work."

"We don't need your services tonight," Tim told We Sa and Staufo.

This was the way it had to be. The other members of the family escorted Staufo and We Sa out the front door and onto their horses. We Sa waved at them with the fingers of her left hand, and the two riders were gone. The tears in their eyes were not distinguishable from the raindrops that were falling on their ponchos and dripping down their cheeks.

Inside the cabin there was a flurry of activity to place all the foodstuffs, cooking gear, ammunition, water bags, canteens, sleeping gear, medicine pack, and the sacks that would hold grass for the horses at their designated place on the floor of the cabin. Anything that they left behind would be taken to the Parker farm tonight by Bixby and Tim.

An unexpected Renwe showed up a half-an-hour after Staufo and We Sa left—he was supposed to go directly to the Parker farm after work, but he decided to come back to the cabin and help load the horses for the trip east.

Arnest, Jean, and Chin did not want to load the gear onto their horses too early—they didn't want any of the neighbors to discover that they were leaving. So there were three hours that had to pass before they could make the final arrangements for the trip east.

🍁   🍁   🍁

An hour later Bixby thought he spotted some unusual movement behind the corral, so he and Howey left the cabin and circled around the corral from two directions. A few minutes later they came back with bad news: There was a miner in the woods, and he was watching everything the Simmons were doing.

He might be a spy for American Mining. They couldn't afford to have him running loose, so what should be done?

Arnest knew that the easiest thing to do was to go out in the woods and capture the man, but then what do you do with him? You couldn't just tie the man to a tree because he might get away in just a few minutes and tell the whole settlement what was going on at the Simmons cabin.

What to do? Bixby decided that they should do nothing for the time being, but they should capture him close to midnight and make sure he couldn't give any warning to the people in the neighborhood when everyone left the cabin.

So they waited for two hours. The rains had stopped, and there was music coming from the general direction of Sally Jo's saloon. They even heard a few fireworks. The big party at the saloon had started on time, and hopefully everyone would be there.

Suddenly there was a knock on the door and everyone froze. Howey opened the door a tiny bit to see who it was. It was Herman.

Herman was in good spirits. He shook the rain off his poncho and told them, "Mrs. Timmons told me to tell you that the big party had been moved inside the saloon because of the rain, but the party is still on."

"We have a problem, Herman," Arnest explained. "There is someone out there in the back of the property that is watching our every move. We don't know what to do with him."

Herman thought for a minute or two, and then came up with a plan. "You all go and capture this man," he said. "Tie him up good and tight and blindfold him so he can't see anything. Then drape him over my horse. I'll take him to a good spot that will keep him occupied for the rest of the evening. But you must remember, do not speak my name while I have him, else he will know who I am. Don't say a word."

That seemed like a good plan, so Howey and Bixby went out the cabin door again to search for their neighborhood 'snoop'. It didn't take them very long to catch him because he was soaked with rain and he made no effort to run away.

They tied him up, blindfolded him, and draped him over Herman's horse. Then they went inside to tell Herman that the man was ready to travel.

"Good," Herman responded. "Now I'll take him to the far edge of the cemetery where there's a huge gravestone. The gravestone rests on three short pillars and there is a stone ledge at the top that is supposed to make it easy to read the inscription on the big stone. Anyway, I'll handcuff him to the center pillar and he can listen to the music coming from the party. The ledge will keep the rain off him so he won't get pneumonia out there. Then, early in the morning I'll arrange for someone to come by the grave marker and discover him. If the party is still going then we will entertain him royally at the bar."

With that explanation, Herman was off into the darkness in silence, leading his horse through the path to the graveyard.

Sally Jo had given Chin a pocket watch so he would know when to make his move toward the jail. According to that pocket watch, Tim, Chin, and Arnest should be at the back door to the jail in twenty minutes. It took ten minutes to get there in good weather, and maybe fifteen minutes in a rain.

Howey, Bixby, and Renwe began loading the gear on the horses that were chosen for the trip east. Arnest's old stallion was one of the chosen. The three men walked briskly to the new jail. There were no horses tied to the hitching post in front, which was a good sign. They stayed close to the edge of the tree line and trudged through the standing water. When they reached the back of the jail there was music coming loudly from Sally Jo's saloon, but no one was in sight. As Sally Jo had said, there was no moon at all.

Tim placed the master key in the back door and the lock moved silently to extract the bolt. There was a squeak as they opened the door, but only one squeak. Tim entered the jail and found Ho and Kim standing at the cell door. He walked past them silently to check on the jail guard, Deputy Klink. Klink was fast asleep on the cot at the front of the jail.

Then he returned to the cell block. He put the master key in the cell lock and it too opened. Success! As Ho and Kim were passing through the back door, Tim relocked their cell.

Then, without warning, there was a loud banging at the front door. Someone was shouting 'let me in', 'let me in', at the top of their lungs. Tim raced to the front of the jail. Klink was still asleep on the bunk, and a bottle of whiskey was lying beside him, partially corked. Tim didn't know what to do—the man who was screaming about coming into the jail might wake up Klink, and then there would be problems.

So Tim quickly ran to the jail guard's station and unlocked the front door with the master key. An old miner was there, and he was angry. "What took you so long?" he asked Tim.

"What do you want, Sir?" Tim asked. The miner retorted with "I want a place to sleep. The Deputy said I could sleep here tonight because I got all wet, and I don't want to catch pneumonia."

Tim immediately helped him into the jail, relocked the front door, and led him carefully to the back cell where Ho and Kim had been. The miner didn't seem to notice Deputy Klink. Tim unlocked the cell and gave the miner the blankets on the lower bunk. The old man took the blankets, covered himself, and was sound asleep in two minutes. Tim relocked the cell.

He looked back at Deputy Klink—he was still sound asleep. He took the whiskey bottle and emptied it on the floor as he walked toward the back of the jail. Then he stepped outside and locked the back door of the jail. He threw the whiskey bottle into the outhouse slit and closed the door.

Arnest, Chin, Ho, and Kim were all standing there in the rain, waiting for him. "Is something wrong?" Chin asked.

"I had to let a guy come in the front door of the jail and go to sleep in the cell," Tim told them. "He said one of the Deputies told him he could sleep in the jail for the night because he was soaked and wet. He's already asleep in the cell."

The group looked at one another, and then trotted back to the cabin, trying to step around the growing pools of water. When they got there, there was no time to exchange hugs and congratulations. It was time to head East. The men put on their sidearms and their ponchos and mounted their horses. There were ten horses saddled up and ready to leave for Truckee Pass.

Jean quietly led the way out of the neighborhood. She and Arnest had rehearsed the route, following the trail toward Truckee, and it was well that they did because the night was pitch black. Arnest brought up the rear. They passed no one on the trail through the entire night, and rode for seven hours straight, until the sun came up. The sky was filled with dark clouds that almost obliterated the sun. The horses seemed to be in good shape, so the five continued for another six hours, and then stopped beside a small mountain stream. They had started a gradual climb, so they knew they were headed into the mountains. Bixby had given Arnest his compass—"Just in case you get lost somewhere along the way," he told Arnest. Arnest took the compass out, laid it on a rock, and confirmed that they were headed east and a little north—toward Truckee.

❧   ❧   ❧

The group who had remained at the cabin had some adventures of their own. Bixby enjoyed the music that continued to come from Sally Jo's saloon, so he wanted to stop by and try a little of Sally Jo's free booze before they headed for the Parker farm. Tim and Howey didn't like the idea at all, but Bixby insisted that he would only be there a few minutes.

So, reluctantly, the group of four (Bixby, Howey, Tim, and Renwe) sauntered up to the saloon and hitched their horses to the rail in front. Howey and Bixby were the first to enter the swinging front door, and in about ten seconds they did a quick turnaround and came out the swinging front door. Tim and Renwe didn't understand what was going on, so they carefully made their way into the saloon. Howey immediately pointed out to them the presence of a tall, skinny man sitting in the center of the room with blankets wrapped around him. He was joining in the singing of 'Red River Valley', which was Herman's favorite song. Herman sat across from the man and he immediately frowned at Bixby and Howey. He motioned to them to leave the saloon with his right arm while he sang and drank with his left arm.

Bixby and Howey got the message—this looked like the miner that they had captured behind the corral earlier in the evening and Herman had tied to the grave marker in the cemetery. This was not the time to join in the merriment.

"At least we know we didn't give him pneumonia," Bixby mentioned as they headed out the front door.

They noticed the Sheriff and his wife sitting at a blackjack table, and next to them was Sally Jo Timmons. Sally spotted Bixby and stood up. She said something to the Rogers, excused herself, and then came to the front door of the saloon. The four men were already removing their animals from the hitching post.

Sally Jo approached them, came very close, and got right to the point. "How did it go?" she asked.

"Our guests are well on their way to their appointed place," Bixby told her.

Sally Jo looked at the watch that she kept clipped to her bodice, and announced, "I guess they have been on their way for over an hour now."

The men all nodded in agreement.

Sally Jo looked at Renwe and asked a favor: "The next time you pass through these parts, please give me a mailing address for your folks in the Kansas Territory. I would like to write to them and thank them for all they have done for this town."

Renwe agreed, and the men began their trip to the Parker farm. The rains subsided, and it was close to sunrise before they reached the farm. They were delayed for over two hours because one of the tributaries of the Sacramento River had overflowed its borders and it wasn't safe to cross—not even with a horse. Bixby's mules weren't too keen about the crossing either.

🍁   🍁   🍁

The next morning there was no way to tell how far Arnest and his group had traveled east, but they knew it would be at least one more day before they reached the Truckee Pass.

Meanwhile, Arnest and the group had reached the hidden box canyon in the pass where the Paiute Indians found apples. They pulled into the apple grove and set up camp for the night. The horses were exhausted by the constant rain and the slippery trail they were following. "Tomorrow we may have to walk the horses most of the way to the Truckee Meadows," Arnest announced. "But even if we walk all the way, we'll be out of California in eight hours or so." Everyone knew that they were close to the pass.

❧   ❧   ❧

The following morning, when they awoke, they felt the touch of snowflakes against their faces. This was a gentle snow, a preview of big snows to come. They ate quickly, knowing that their next night would be spent at the Truckee Meadows. Then they packed up and headed through the pass.

On November 1, 1851, they reached the Truckee Meadows. They had no intention of remaining at the Meadows for any long period of time, but they were concerned about the next leg of the trip—finding the Humboldt Sink and the river. Arnest and Jean missed not having Tim for this trek, because he was the one who always checked the horses and shifted loads so a weary horse could get some rest. About the time they were ready to leave the Meadows they saw a small group of Indians headed their way, coming from the north. When the Indians got within a hundred yards, Jean and Arnest breathed a sigh of relief—these were the same Paiutes that had led them through the Truckee Pass going west two years earlier.

When the Paiutes approached, the Chief recognized Arnest and Jean. He approached them directly and showed them the fine Morgan mare he was riding. The badly hobbled mare had been nursed back to health and she looked great. "It's too bad Tim is not here," Arnest thought to himself. "He would have liked to see how well they have treated this horse."

The Chief again pointed to two of the Braves close to him, and they moved to positions on the flanks of the Cherokee party. The one brave came close to Arnest and asked in a deep voice, "Salt Lake City?"

Jean overhead the words, and she returned quickly with "Yes, yes, Salt Lake City. Salt Lake City!"

The Chief had no smoked meat to offer to the travelers this time—the desert animals had hibernated for the winter. But he handed them a food that they all knew about—jerky.

Then Jean turned to Arnest and said to him, "Arnest, it is time for you to give a real gift to your brothers who make their lives in this terrible land. If you're going to give a gift, make it a real gift!

Arnest understood completely what his wife was saying. He dismounted from his aging stallion, carefully removed the saddle, water bags, and saddlebags from the animal, placed them on his pack horse, and walked slowly over to the Chief. When he got there he took the reins of that beautiful animal that had transported him for almost twenty years, and handed them to the Chief. There were tears in Arnest's eyes, and tears in the eyes of the Paiute Chief also. They were kindred spirits at that moment in time.

CHAPTER 15

Return to Fort Lupton

Chin Zhou was determined to get Arnest and Jean to pass through New Fort Kearney before they continued south to Fort Lupton. He argued that time had come to a standstill now—that the trip to Fort Lupton by way of the California Trail was only 200 miles further than if they cut all the corners of the Rocky Mountains and attempted to return via the Cache Le Poudre.

He was 'blowing smoke' of course; the increased trek would be well over 300 miles through New Fort Kearney. But there was plenty of time to discuss this issue because spring was a long way away. The big issue right now was that they were passing through a desert that could be filled in the winter with up to twenty feet of snow (coming from the northwest). Bixby had told them all about this 'great basin' when they left Salt Lake City headed west.

The trip back through the Paiute desert, the Humboldt River, the Salt Lake Desert, and finally to Salt Lake City pretty well wore them out. Their animals were exhausted also. The riders caught the last of the scorching heat in the day and the first of the northwesterly winds that pulled the nighttime temperature well below freezing. They arrived in Salt Lake City in early January 1852. It was obvious that they could go no further until spring came.

Jean wrote letters to Eileen and Marcy in the Cherokee Nation and to Renwe and Staufo in California, informing them that the 'return' party had faced more heat and cold than they could handle, so they were camping in Salt Lake City for the time being. The big snows were coming soon.

The five adults had enough money to afford the finest hotel in Salt Lake City, but that was not the plan. All five wanted land to farm and water to irrigate. The Nebraska and Kansas Territories was the answer to their dreams.

They were pleased to find that there were some small 'shacks' for rent on the west side of town. Every year there were emigrants who moved too slowly across the plains and the wagonmasters were forced to keep the wagon train in Salt Lake City until spring came. The man who rented a shack to them suggested that they look for work in downtown Salt Lake City, which was less than two miles from where they were staying. He also told them that the corral that adjoined the shack had been broken into several times and it needed rework. "This may be a holy city to many who live here," he commented, "but this town also has its share of horse thieves."

The families who lived in these shacks were of two completely different 'ilks'—those traveling west, either by way of the California Trail or the Oregon Trail, and those traveling east, which was a tiny number compared to the westbound emigrants. The Oregon Trail wagon trains had come almost one hundred miles south of their planned trek to stay in Salt Lake City for the winter—their wagonmasters chose not to risk the lives of the entire party in the harsh snows of the great basin between Salt Lake City and Oregon City, a distance well over a thousand miles.

The 'party of five' who were returning from California knew that they dare not discuss the fact that they had participated in the '1849 gold rush' with anyone around them, because some thief would overhear their words and visit them at a time they least expected.

Arnest got a job repairing iron-rimmed wagon wheels, a trade that he had picked up by watching Tim Wisnant and Staufo at work in California. Jean refused to be the one who stayed at home (and guarded the shack) this time, so she got a job in a large downtown store that sold ladies' clothing. Her customers were amazed at how much she knew about what women were wearing in Monterrey and San Francisco, California. One would have thought that these two California cities were the new 'Paris' of the far western-American world.

It was at this store that she found out how much the downtown had improved since the Cherokees passed through just two years earlier. A tiny English bank had set up for business near the city center—they liked to intimate that they were part of the 'Bank of England'. Well, maybe they were and maybe they weren't, but Jean and Arnest rented a 'box' at the bank and placed most of their gold there. Chin refused to participate in such a risky business, so the task of guarding the shack fell to his family, most of the time. Once Jean and Arnest put their gold in the bank there wasn't much that could be stolen from them at the shack—except for the fine horses they owned.

The corral that adjoined the shack wasn't made to hold ten horses, but it had to do. Additional fence posts were placed in the void spaces of the corral, the gate was reinforced, and the Simmons did something they had never done before—they put barbed wire across the top of the corral. When spring came these animals would be expected to climb one more mountain range and travel at least 600 miles, so it was necessary to keep them in 'training'. The horses were ridden every third day, at least ten miles.

Chin decided that he and his two boys would split their gold three ways, and they carried the gold with them all the time. The secret to keeping the gold was this: don't ever go out at night and don't ever be alone. Dad didn't have to preach these ideas too much to Ho and Kim because they both knew what had happened to Yang when he found himself alone in the middle of the night in Coloma.

They got jobs delivering lumber to places all around the city, and they arranged for two of the three to work on any given day. One person was always at the shack.

But you must travel part of the time in the dark when February and March come—there isn't that much daylight. So every morning Arnest and Jean traveled to her work first, and then Arnest took both horses to his place of business (which was full of people working on wagons and had a large corral). Then, at the end of the day he would go back to Jean's place of business downtown and the two of them would ride together to the shack.

In the middle of May the group of five loaded their horses, bought fresh ammunition, and began retracing their steps through Fort Bridger and points east. The bank in Salt Lake City charged them $12.00 to keep their gold through the winter. Arnest and Jean wanted to appease Chin and go with him all the way to New Fort Kearney, but it just couldn't be. For one thing, they didn't know how long their horses would hold-up on this return trip. So the two groups separated at Fort Bridger: The Chins went up to the famed 'South Pass' and made their way to Fort Laramie and finally New Fort Kearney. The Simmons stayed along the Kansas Territory—Nebraska Territory line and turned due south at the little village now known as 'Cheyenne'.

Once the Simmons arrived at Fort Lupton they were able to buy the land that they wanted on the South Platte River. They were able to tell Mr. and Mrs. Wisnant about some of Tim's adventures, and reported that he was still a bachelor, so far as they knew. He was the only blacksmith in Coloma, California. Pat gave Irene Tim's mailing address in Sacramento. The Wisnants ended up selling their land to Arnest and Jean and moving south to a place called Auraria. Mr. Wisnant was finally going to get his chance to build stone fireplaces.

Renwe continued his bachelor ways, or so his letters indicated. He kept a close track on his little brother and reported that Staufo and We Sa had settled in Sacramento, which was now firmly entrenched as the capitol city of California. She was teaching school and working on a teaching job at the local university, while Staufo continued to design and build wagons for Mr. Studebaker.

Jean wrote several letters to Bixby and Howey, and received very few in return. Staufo was able to confirm that the two went into the grape-growing business and they loved it.

Sally Jo Timmons wrote the longest letter that she had probably written in her life about a year after the Simmons and Zhous escaped from California. She accounted for everybody: The Sheriff and his wife had survived the jail break and he was now running for the State Legislature; Bixby and Howey were settling into the winery business, Sally Jo had given the little yellow house to Herman and he had promptly found a bride among the new arrivals in town, and Billie Beavers finally got up the nerve to propose to Sally Jo Timmons (which she immediately accepted). They were going to move to San Francisco because

Coloma was fast becoming a 'has-been' town where there wasn't much excitement. "You just can't mine gold all your life," Sally Jo commented.

She also filled in some of the details about what happened the night of the big jail break. Deputy Klink finally woke up when one of the other Deputies brought an unruly miner to the jail. There were two empty cells so they put the miner in the first cell, and everyone went back to sleep.

Then, when Klink woke up about daybreak, he realized that the snoring noises coming from the third cell were not the kinds of noises that two young Chinese men made. When he checked the cell he realized that he only had one prisoner in the last cell, not two. He immediately sounded the alarm, but there was no indication of a jailbreak.

The universal signal to report a jailbreak was to fire three shots in the air, and this is exactly what Klink did. The first person to reach the jail was Sergeant Beavers, and he immediately called for reinforcements. It had been raining on and off all night, so there were no tracks to follow. The decision was made that the two Chinese men had hightailed it for San Francisco, so a posse was formed quickly and they rode west to Sacramento.

Two days later they returned with information that the prisoners had escaped and all that could be done was to post notices for their arrest in Sacramento, San Francisco, Hangtown, etc. The Sheriff posted a $200 reward for their capture, and the Eldorado County Sheriff's Office waited for a lead.

At the time that Sally Jo was writing, the $200 reward was still out there, and there were no takers. Some people in Hangtown demanded an investigation, but the investigation got nowhere because there was no way the prisoners could have escaped. The old miner who had spent the night in the same cell that Ho and Kim were placed in originally told the investigators that he thought that the person who opened the front door of the jail to let him in was not a human being—he was some kind of a devil. He figured that the Devil had come that night to take Ho and Kim Zhou directly to Hell for their evil deeds. So what was left to investigate?

There was no mention in the investigation about what had happened to Chin Zhou or his daughter, We Sa, but it was noted that the old man had sold their claim a few days before they disappeared. Nothing was ever written about the Simmons family.

Epilogue

It took Jean almost eight years to convince her daughters, Eileen and Marcy, along with their husbands and children, that the Kansas Territory was the place to be. She accomplished this feat by outright bribes, giving both families large tracts of land along the South Platte River as these tracts became available. It was a difficult decision for the daughters and their families to make because, once they left the Cherokee Nation Territory, they forfeited their rights to ever live there again. They owned none of the land. The daughters and their families made the move to the Kansas Territory in 1860, just a few months before the outbreak of the Civil War.

The land that the Simmons and their children owned along the South Platte River is significant today because most of it is used to raise barley and hops for a German emigrant family led by Adolph Coors.

The Zhou family remained in Nebraska until New Fort Kearney was closed many years later, then they emigrated south to a tiny suburb of Auraria, Colorado. The suburb was later named 'Denver'.

Just two years after the 'golden spike' was driven at Promontory, Utah Territory, Jean and Arnest drove their buckboard to Cheyenne and rode the iron horse all the way to Sacramento, where they were met by Staufo, We Sa, and three grandchildren who had never met their grandparents before. It was a happy reunion.

RPB, December 2005

About the Author

Richard Braden is a retired Army/Air Force person, an aeronautical engineer who worked for NASA and Lockheed, and a university professor who taught in Ohio and Colorado. He found out about the 'Simmons' family in this story by chance, while reading some of the old documents about Douglas County, Colorado in the period before Colorado became a territory (1840–1861). No one knows their real family name, but they spent some time in this county, and then headed for the gold fields in 1849 via Fort Bridger and Salt Lake City.

After their stay at Sutter's Mill they marched on into history. They must have been a hardy, determined family that always kept the primary goal in mind—success for all members of the family.

Richard Braden can be contacted at 'rbraden@comcast.net'.

1360198